# THE YOUNG CAPTIVES

A Story of Judah and Babylon

Erasmus W. Jones

1ˢᵗ WORLD
LIBRARY
Literary Society

# The Young Captives
## A Story of Judah and Babylon

Erasmus W. Jones

© 1st World Library – Literary Society, 2005
PO Box 2211
Fairfield, IA 52556
www.1stworldlibrary.org
First Edition

LCCN: 2004195611

Softcover ISBN: 1-4218-0432-8
Hardcover ISBN: 1-4218-0332-1
eBook ISBN: 1-4218-0532-4

Purchase *"The Young Captives"*
as a traditional bound book at:
www.1stWorldLibrary.org/purchase.asp?ISBN=1-4218-0432-8

1st World Library Literary Society is a nonprofit
organization dedicated to promoting literacy by:

- Creating a free internet library accessible from any computer worldwide.
- Hosting writing competitions and offering book publishing scholarships.

***The Young Captives***
*contributed by Tim, Ed & Rodney*
*in support of*
*1st World Library Literary Society*

# PREFACE.

This volume is the fruit of my leisure hours; and those hours in the life of a pastor are not very abundant. That the story has suffered from this, I do not believe. Whatever its defects may be, they are not owing to "the pressure of other duties." So, dear reader, if this little work proves a failure, let not that deep calamity be attributed to any lack but the lack of ability in the author.

The semi-fictitious style of the writing, while displeasing to some, will be well-pleasing to others. "What I have written I have written;" perhaps in a way peculiar to myself. I know of some who could write charming books on this subject in a very different and perhaps a far superior style; but these I dare not try to imitate. I must write in my own way. It may be inferior to the way of others; but then it is much better to move around on your own limbs, even if they are rather "short metre," than to parade abroad on stilts in mid-air.

In the colloquies, I have not thought it best to follow strictly the Oriental style. However pleasing this might have been to some, I am well persuaded that it could not meet the approbation of the generality of readers; and as the great design of the work is to bear with weight upon some of the corrupt usages and wicked policies of the present day, I thought it advisable to shape the phraseology in conformity with modern usages.

In the prosecution of this work, I have consulted the following authorities: Josephus, Rollins' "Ancient History," Smith's "Sacred Annals," "Daniel, a Model for Young Men," by Dr. Scott, Clarke's, Henry's, Scott's, and Benson's Commentaries; with some other smaller works.

In following the "Youths of Judah" through their various trials, at home and in a land of strangers, I have received much genuine pleasure and lasting profit; and that the reader, likewise, may be greatly pleased and benefited, is the sincere desire of his unworthy servant, Erasmus W. Jones.

# CHAPTER I.

A CLASH of swords and the cries of excited men resounded through the streets of the city. Two guardsmen were endeavoring to disarm and arrest a number of boisterous youths. The latter, evidently young men of good social position, had been singing bacchanalian songs and otherwise conducting themselves in a manner contrary to the spirit of orderliness which King Josiah was striving to establish in Jerusalem. The youths were intoxicated, and, when the two officers sought to restrain them, they drew swords and made a reckless attack on the guardians of the peace.

Although the latter were outnumbered, they were courageous and skillful men, and soon had three of the party disarmed, accomplishing this without bloodshed. The fourth and last of the marauders, a handsome and stalwart young man apparently about twenty-one years of age, although at first desirous of keeping out of the melee, sprang to the aid of his companions. He cleverly tripped one of the watchmen and grappled with the other in such a way that the officer could not use his sword arm. This fierce onslaught gave the other members of the party new courage, and they joined in the battle again. The conflict might then have been settled in favor of the lawless party but for an unexpected circumstance. As one of the guardsmen gave a signal calling for reinforcements, the second made a desperate attempt to throw his young antagonist to the ground, and, as they struggled, his face came in proximity to that of the offending youth. He uttered an exclamation of surprise.

"Ezrom! Ezrom!" cried he; "don't add crime to your other follies! Do you realize what you are doing? See how you are about to bring disgrace upon your relatives. Make haste away from this place before the reinforcements come, or nothing will save you from the dungeon. I beseech you in the name of the king and your beloved family!"

Instantly the plea had its effect. The young man drew back, and, hastily uttering a few words to his companions, led them away before they could be recognized by the gathering crowd.

"The officer is a loyal friend of our house," the youth explained, "and we have him to thank for getting us out of this trouble, temporarily at least. But the affair has attracted enough notice so that there is sure to be an inquiry to-morrow, and I for one will put the city of my birth behind me before the dawn of day. The son of Salome and the nephew of King Josiah will never again bring disgrace upon those he loves. To-night I flee to parts unknown, and bitter indeed will be the punishment of those of you who are apprehended for our offenses."

In the vicinity of the Temple stood a beautiful dwelling. From outward appearances one would readily conclude that the inmates of that fair abode were not common personages. Wealth and taste were shown on every hand. To this house, in the heart of Jerusalem, came the young man who had rendered himself so conspicuous in the quarrel with the guard. He reached the place by a circuitous route and hastily entered. Although the hour was late two Hebrew maidens of rare beauty awaited his coming. They were in a state of anxious solicitude for the return of their erring brother, whose conduct of late had been such as to cause the most intense anxiety on the part of the pious household, for Ezrom belonged to the nobility of Judah and was a blood relation of the reigning monarch. Seeing his excited countenance, the sisters understood that something unusual had befallen him, and the elder of the two sprang to his side.

"What calamity has occurred to you, my dear brother?" she cried.

"Be calm, sweet Serintha," he replied, "and I will tell you all."

He then informed his sisters that with his three friends he had been guilty of taking up arms against the authorities - a crime punished with great severity.

As Ezrom and his young men companions were connected with families of high station in Jerusalem, even having royal blood in their veins, they had the privilege of carrying weapons and were in the habit of going armed with swords. This unfortunate custom had only served in the end to get them into serious trouble, and Ezrom for one felt compelled to leave home during the night.

These startling disclosures brought from both of his sisters a cry of agony. They implored him to remain, promising to exert every influence to save him from punishment.

Ezrom's mind was firmly made up, however, and he declared that he never would face the impending exposure. He gathered together a few articles of clothing while his sisters followed him from room to room with painful sobs. He was soon ready. His younger sister, Monroah, fell on his neck in a paroxysm of grief. Ezrom could utter but a few broken words when he essayed to bid them farewell. His favorite harp stood by his side.

"Take this, my sweet Monroah," he said, in trembling accents, "and whenever thy hand shall strike its chords of melody remember that thou art loved with all the strong affection of a brother's heart. And now, in the presence of Jehovah I make the solemn vow that from this hour I shall reform my ways."

He then kissed his beloved sisters, and, with burning brow and tear-dimmed eyes, rushed from his father's house and away to a land of strangers.

# CHAPTER II.

NEARLY a quarter of a century had rolled away, and again the city of Jerusalem was ablaze with light and social gayety. But vastly different was the moral tone of the government. The good King Josiah had been called to rest, and his profligate son Jehoiakim was on the throne. Nightly the walls of the royal palace rang with the sound of high revelry. Laughter and drunken song echoed through every part of the proud edifice. Jehoiakim, following the example of some of his predecessors, did that which was evil in the sight of the Lord and filled the Holy City with his foul abominations. His counselors also lived in forgetfulness of the God of Israel. They flattered the king's vanity and encouraged his excesses. Pride and infidelity promenaded together. Crimes of the darkest hue were being perpetrated with official sanction, and, although God's prophets had the courage to rebuke the sinful rulers and warn them of their fearful doom, the moral standard of the city went lower and lower.

The night was serene and calm. The glorious orb shone brightly in the eastern skies and shed her silvery beams on the glassy lakes of Judea. In the clear moonbeams, those lofty towers of spotless white stood forth in majestic grandeur on the walls of the great metropolis. Nature, with smiles of lovely innocence on her fair countenance, was hushed to sweet repose; but not so the busy thousands that thronged the wide thorough-fares of Jerusalem. This day was one of the anniversaries of Jehoiakim's reign, and at an early hour the city presented a scene of excitement. The king's vanity provided everything requisite for a general display; and, although far from being loved by his numerous subjects, yet because they could eat, drink, and be merry at the expense of others, the streets of Jerusalem were thronged with those who cared far more for the gratification of their appetites than they did for their vain sovereign.

The royal palace was thronged with the rich, the great, the gay, and the giddy. Unholy excitement ran high. Wines and strong drinks flowed freely. Flattery without measure was poured into the ears of the king. "Long live Jehoiakim!" echoed from a thousand voices. The prophets of the Most High, who prophesied evil against Jerusalem, were ridiculed and laughed to scorn; and those few persons of influence who regarded them in a favorable light were made the subjects of their keenest sarcasm and their most insulting wit. It was about the third hour of the night. The king's heart was merry with wine. A thousand of Judah's nobles, with their wives, their sons, and their daughters, sat at the banquet table. Suddenly a voice, deep and solemn as the grave, was heard below, as if in the garden at the rear of the palace, crying, "Woe unto Jehoiakim, King of Judah! Woe! Woe to the Holy City!" The sound was of an unearthly nature. The assembly heard it, the king heard it. For a moment, all was still. Again the same deep minor sound was clearly heard. "Woe unto Jehoiakim, King of Judah! Woe! Woe unto the Holy City!"

"Seize the accursed wretch!" rang through the

great apartment.

The king's countenance was flushed with anger, while he cried, "Who is this vile dog that dares insult the King of Judah? Let the abominable one be dragged into my presence and then receive his instant doom!"

A thorough search was made for the mysterious author of the confusion; guards and sentinels ran to and fro. Every corner of the enclosures was thoroughly examined, but all in vain. No trace could be found of the unwelcome herald. After a short interval, the agitation subsided and the company was again in the midst of wild revelry and merriment. The king endeavored to be merry; but the peculiar deep tone of that messenger of woe still sounded in his ears; and, with all his efforts, he could not forget it. In the midst of his depravity and wickedness, he still at times had some dread of that God whom he daily insulted. He sought to drown his unpleasant thoughts in mixed wines, but the King of Judah felt a presentiment of some awful calamity near at hand. With desperation he struggled against it, and joined in the boisterous laugh and merry song.

# CHAPTER III.

HIGHER and higher ran the excitement of the banquet-room. Loud peals of laughter broke from the merry throng. Musical instruments poured forth rich strains of melody. Jehoiakim was complimented on every hand, but the law of God was ridiculed.

Jehoiakim sat on a magnificent throne, gilded over with pure gold. A large number of war officers sat near him. A royal herald passed through the throng, crying, "Listen to the oration of Sherakim! Listen to the oration of Sherakim!" Soon silence was obtained, and Sherakim the Orator stood before the vast concourse, and began:

"Princes and Nobles of Judah! With merry hearts, we assemble from different parts of the kingdom to hail this festal day - the eleventh anniversary of the reign of our illustrious sovereign. Ye will not think it strange, nor consider it affectation, when I assure you that I tremble beneath the weight of honor conferred upon me at this time.

"The death of King Josiah, as ye well know, threw a partial gloom over Judah. Not because all of us considered his measures expedient and prudent, but because he was our king, and undoubtedly honest in his intentions, amid all his imperfections. Let the infirmities and mistakes of past monarchs be buried in their graves. We are not here to mourn over the past, but rather to rejoice in the present. We are here assembled to congratulate one another on the unprecedented happiness that flows to the nation from the reign of the truly illustrious sovereign that now adorns the throne of Judah. The faults and deficiencies of other-day kings are more than made up to the nation in the bright reign of the most excellent Jehoiakim. We do not expect that even the superior administration of our matchless monarch will suit the tastes and desires of weak-minded and superstitious men. The King of Judah, with all his superior powers, is not capable of satisfying the unreasonable demands of those deluded creatures who are yet too numerous in our midst. What good can result to anyone from spending half his time in yonder Temple, and there going through a long list of senseless ceremonies, with sad and melancholy looks?

"Princes and Nobles of Judah! We rejoice together under the happy reign of a king who looks at those things with calm disdain, and smiles at the foolishness and darkness of other ages. Let us, therefore, banish gloom and enjoy life. Let deluded visionaries bow their heads, disfigure their countenances, and utter their plaintive moans; but let men stand erect, with joyful countenances and merry hearts! They tell us that Jerusalem is in danger; and they dwell with solemn emphasis on what they please to call 'forgetfulness of God.' They tell us that the Chaldeans are about to besiege the city, and take it! This old story will answer well to terrify shallow brains and young children; but, with men of sense, it will receive that silent contempt which it deserves. Let the citizens of Judah give themselves no uneasiness on account of the silly harangues of a wild and deluded fanatic who is a more fit subject to be confined with unruly lunatics than to be heeded as a teller of future events. However, I would not advise severity towards the followers of old Jeremiah. They are rather to be pitied than blamed. As long as they keep their delusion within their own circles, we shall let them alone; but let them be careful that they step not too far and disturb the happiness and enjoyment of others. Among themselves, let them talk about the 'Law of their God,' to their hearts' content; but as for us, we know of no higher law than the law of our king - the edicts of our grand sovereign. To him, and him alone, we pledge our undivided fidelity. Trusting in the King of Judah, we cheerfully go forward, and bid defiance to every foe. In conclusion, I have only to say, Long live Jehoiakim on the throne of Judah!"

"Long live Jehoiakim!" echoed throughout the assembly. The king bowed and smiled, and Sherakim the Orator's countenance gave evidence that he considered his efforts as crowned with success. All was again hilarity and mirth. The wine passed freely around. Shouts of laughter rang through the spacious hall. A strange person entered the apartment, at that end opposite to the spot where the king sat on his golden throne. His singular appearance arrested the attention of all present. The stranger had passed the meridian of life. His figure was tall, his countenance striking. Deep solemnity rested on his visage, which presented a very strange contrast to the countenances that surrounded him. With a slow but firm step, he walked through the long passage and stood in the presence of Jehoiakim.

The vast assembly was soon hushed to silence, and

spellbound from curiosity. Sherakim the Orator gazed on the king. The king, with an angry brow, gazed on the stranger. The stranger, in return, cast a withering glance on the king, and stood in his presence with form erect and fearless. He lifted his hand on high, and thus addressed the monarch:

"Hear the word of the Lord, O King of Judah, that sittest upon the throne of David. Woe unto him that buildeth his house by unrighteousness, and his chambers by wrong; that useth his neighbor's service without wages, and giveth him not for his work. Did not thy father eat and drink and do justice, and was it not well with him? He judged the cause of the poor, and then it was well with him. 'Was not this to know me?' saith the Lord. But thine eyes and thine heart are not but for thy covetousness, for to shed innocent blood, and for oppression and for violence. Therefore, thus saith the Lord concerning Jehoiakim, 'He shall be buried with the burial of an ass, drawn and cast forth beyond the gates of Jerusalem.'"

The stranger turned his back on Jehoiakim, and with the same slow, firm step, he marched through; and although the king in a rage gave orders for his arrest, there was none to lift a finger against the man of God. He was gone! and the assembly was left gazing in mute astonishment at one another. Such was the unearthly aspect of that mysterious stranger, that even the great flow of spirit was not proof against its effects. The deep tones of his mournful predictions reached their ears and even their hearts. In spite of their abominations and infidelity, they felt that there was a divinity in that awful voice of warning, and for a short period, at least, their hearts throbbed with guilty emotions of fear. Many a proud daughter of Judah trembled and turned pale, as she gazed on the solemn visage of the uninvited stranger, and as she listened to the deeptoned eloquence that fell from his lips. Others there were who felt a strange throbbing of heart, but each one vied with his fellow to hide his real feelings; and soon, by a show of bravado, the concourse fell back to the usual hilarity, marked by more than an ordinary degree of unholy wit, and blasphemous sarcasm.

# CHAPTER IV.

THE night was far advanced, and there were indications that the great festival was drawing to a close. The last feature expected was an address from the king. The hour appointed had arrived, and expectation ran high, but Jehoiakim made not his appearance. At last Sherakim appeared before the vast audience, and commenced an apology for the absence of the monarch in the following strain:

"Princes and Nobles of Judah! It is with heartfelt regret that I am compelled to convey to you the painful intelligence that our illustrious sovereign, owing to illness, will not be able to deliver the royal address. This no one can regret more than your unworthy servant. Is it any wonder that - "

Just at this time, the king himself, with a flushed countenance and a very unsteady step, appeared on the stage. It was glaringly evident to all who were not in the same condition themselves, that the King of Judah was altogether incompetent for that important branch of business which, in despite of the kind remonstrances of his personal friends, he was determined to undertake.

The reader is already aware that the king had been twice disturbed by the dark predictions of the persecuted Jeremiah. In the attempt to throw off his embarrassment, and appear courageous before his friends, he sought relief in mixed wines, of which he partook without restraint. These, in a measure, proved sufficient to stupefy his guilty conscience, but they added to his vanity and self-conceit. Long before the hour arrived for the delivery of the royal address, the King of Judah's conversation amounted to nothing more than drunken babbling.

A number of his most influential courtiers endeavored, with all their tact and ingenuity, to dissuade their sovereign from the attempt, urging that the excitement of the night had already so prostrated him that it would be unsafe for his health to enter again into the uproar of the festive hall. Now, Sherakim had come to the conclusion that their arguments had finally prevailed, and that the king had been comfortably removed to his bed-chamber; hence his remarks, which were cut short by the sudden appearance of the king. Jehoiakim, without any ceremony, commanded the orator to fall back; which command was instantly obeyed. Instead of ascending the throne, as usual, he took the stand that had been vacated by Sherakim, waved his hand, and loudly laughed, while the audience cheered; then, with violent gestures and faltering tongue, he went on:

"Princes and Nobles of Judah! I am here! I tell you I am here! Am I not Jehoiakim, King of Judah? Is not this the glorious reign of my anniversary? Where is the villain that dares to say it is not? Then that is a settled question. I hear no contradiction. Who dares contradict? I hear no reply. Who is afraid of the King of Babylon? If ye know of such an one, bring the cowardly dog to me, and I will take off his head - Ha! ha! ha! Old Jeremiah! Where is he? Ah, I'll soon put him out of the way. Can there be any danger while the King of Babylon is fighting with the King of Egypt?

"Princess and Nobles of Judah! I perceive ye understand your sovereign. We are all safe! He dethroned me three years ago - Ha! ha! ha! Will he do it again? Shall I pay him any more tribute money? Never! I defy his power! And to-morrow I shall punish the enemies of Judah who live in our midst. Tomorrow shall flow rivers of blood!"

The heavy blasts of trumpets were now distinctly heard without, which arrested the king in his drunken speech. A number of officers rose to their feet. A young officer in uniform rushed into the banquet-hall and cried at the top of his voice: "To arms! To arms! To arms, O Judah! The legions of the Chaldeans are approaching the Holy City! To arms! To arms! To arms!" and the officer hurried again into the street. The confusion that ensued was indescribable. Officers ran to and fro in wild haste. Wives and daughters wailed, lamented, and clung to their husbands and fathers in the utmost dismay. Hilarity and mirth were turned into sorrow and bitter lamentations. Those proud and lofty arches that had so lately rung to the sound of the merry song and boisterous laugh, now answered to the distracted cry of the fair daughters of Judah. Thus, in "confusion worse confounded," broke up the great festival of the last anniversary of the reign of Jehoiakim, King of Judah.

The dawn of day presented to the inhabitants of Jerusalem their true and lamentable condition. A portion of the Chaldean army was already encamped on the plains before the city, and nearby the remaining legions were on a rapid march to the same spot. This sudden appearance of the forces of Nebuchadnezzar before the walls of Jerusalem was owing to the King of Judah's refusing to pay the tribute money as agreed on another occasion.

Three years before, the same king, who then reigned jointly with his father, brought his forces before the city, and without any resistance they thought fit to surrender. Jehoiakim was still permitted to reign, but subjected to be a tributary to the King of Babylon. For two years this agreement was adhered to by the King of Judah. On the third, the King of Babylon marched his forces into Egypt, to bring into subjection the revolting inhabitants, whom he had previously conquered. Jehoiakim, trusting that the Egyptians would be able to stand their ground, and, peradventure, prove victorious, thought this a favorable time to throw off the Chaldean yoke; and consequently, scornfully refused to pay the tribute money, and treated the Chaldean ambassador with haughtiness. But, contrary to the expectations of the King of Judah, the Egyptians, when they beheld the powerful legions of the Chaldeans, gave up their rebellion, and promised allegiance to the King of Babylon. Nebuchadnezzar, enraged by the conduct of the King of Judah, ordered his forces in Egypt to march and encamp before the walls of Jerusalem.

Early in the morning of that fatal day, Jehoiakim called together a grand council, in order to deliberate on the best measures to be pursued in the painful emergency. Some advised a strenuous resistance; others said this would be vain - that the city was not able to stand a siege for one month because they were destitute of provisions, and, moreover, the army was in a very imperfect condition. The king thought it advisable to show no resistance, but to treat the King of Babylon with, civility. Finally, the grand council agreed that it was not expedient to resist the entrance of the King of Babylon, and concluded to throw open the gates of the city.

As yet the Chaldeans remained stationary, about thirty furlongs to the south. About the third hour they began to advance, their glittering arms, dazzling in the bright sunbeams, giving them a grand and imposing appearance. The walls of the city were thronged with anxious gazers, and all hearts throbbed with deep and painful anxiety. Nearer and nearer they approached! The rumbling of their war chariots fell heavily on the ear. The heavy hoofs of their spirited chargers made the earth tremble. The loud blasts of their numerous trumpeters were carried on the wings of the wind, while the echoes answered from the lofty towers of ancient Salem. Suddenly the massive gates were thrown open. Then a grand shout from the whole army rent the air. For hours they poured in through the wide portals, and once more the gods of the Gentiles were escorted in triumph through the wide thoroughfares of the "City of the Great King."

# CHAPTER V.

THE King of Judah's treatment of the Chaldean ambassador, in regard to the tribute money, had so exasperated the King of Babylon, that he was determined to chasten his audacity with rigor. This monarch, at this period of his reign, was of rather a mild disposition, but, like his sires before him, a love of conquest had become with him a strong passion.

Three years before, he had dealt with much mildness toward the inhabitants of Jerusalem. On taking the city, he charged his soldiers to show no indignity to the inhabitants, under the severest penalty - which charge was well heeded. Towards Jehoiakim he also evinced a kind disposition. With but few restrictions, he was permitted to reign. Now that Jehoiakim had abused these acts of kindness, had violated solemn obligations, and, in addition to all this, had publicly ridiculed the ambassador, Nebuchadnezzar's indignation was kindled to a flame.

The King of Judah on this occasion, as well as on all other occasions of embarrassment and perplexity, sought relief in mixed wines. These stimulated his courage for the time being, which, being left to its own resources, was of a low order; but, under the effects of these deceitful liquids, he became heroic.

"Jared!" said Jehoiakim, "where is that Sherakim who was so full of fight at the banquet hall last night?"

"As my soul liveth, O king, I know not his whereabouts. I have not seen him since early dawn; and then he appeared to be in haste, and was in no mood for conversation."

"A curse on his cowardly head! I suppose these Chaldeans have put his valor to flight. Jared! how many armed men have we within the royal enclosures?"

"Two hundred of the royal guard, O king, are present - all armed and ready to face death for their illustrious sovereign."

"It is well!" said Jehoiakim, filling his bowl. "Ha, ha, ha! Let the King of Babylon beware of my vengeance? What does the fool desire? The King of Judah is not to be frightened. Jared! where is Sherakim?"

"Sherakim, O king, is not to be found."

"Ah, I had forgotten. Sherakim not to be found! Ha, ha, ha! Sherakim not to be found! The cowardly babbler! Jared, command more wine! Sherakim has fled - he is afraid of a shadow - he has not the courage of a maiden. Have I not known him of old? Did not a thunderstorm always make him cry? Ha, ha, ha! Sherakim the orator! fool! coward!"

"A messenger, O king, from the King of the Chaldeans, desires to be introduced into thy presence. Shall I conduct him to the apartment?"

"Is he alone or accompanied?"

"Accompanied by armed men."

"Let the messenger be admitted, but let the guard remain behind."

The messenger was accordingly ushered into the presence of Jehoiakim.

"And what business of importance has brought thee into the presence of the King of Judah?" asked Jehoiakim, with curling lip.

"I stand in thy presence as a bearer of a message from my sovereign master, King of Babylon."

"Methinks I have seen thee on another occasion."

"And was not my behavior honorable and becoming?"

"Did the King of Judah say otherwise?"

"Yea, otherwise."

"How?"

"By his vile and haughty treatment of the king's ambassador."

"Be sparing with thine insolence, or at this time thou mayest fare far worse."

"The Chaldean ambassador is not to be frightened by idle threats from one who lives at the mercy of his master."

Erasmus W. Jones

"Thinkest thou thyself safe because thou art surrounded with a few soldiers? Knowest thou not that within my call there are hundreds of armed men, ready to execute my will?"

"And knowest thou not that Jerusalem is in the hands of the Chaldeans, and that threescore thousand men of war are stationed in the city?"

"Threescore thousand! But come, sir, what is the message of the King of Babylon to the King of Judah? Let thy words be few."

"Then thou art commanded, without delay, to appear in my master's presence, and there learn his sovereign will concerning thyself and the city."

"Commanded! Ha, ha, ha! Go thy way, and inform thy master that if he desires to see Jehoiakim, King of Judah, he must call at the royal palace, where he may have his desires gratified."

"Then I go. Faithfully will I convey thy answer to my illustrious sovereign."

The minister hastened from the royal palace, to convey to the king the result of the interview, while the King of Judah, waxing more desperate, still applied himself to his cups.

The King of Babylon, on his arrival in Jerusalem, ordered his magnificent royal tent to be pitched in the center of a large square in the very heart of the city. The great body of the army was stationed in another part - the royal guard remaining near the royal tent. From this spot went forth the summons to the King of

Judah to appear in the presence of the King of Babylon.

"Where is his Royal Highness, the King of Judah?" asked Nebuchadnezzar.

"In his palace, O king, indulging in excess of wine, apparently perfectly at ease."

"Is he not forthcoming?" asked the king, with a darkened brow.

"He laughs to scorn thy commands, O king! and wishes to inform thee that if thou hast aught to communicate he may be consulted at his palace."

"By all the gods, the fellow is mad!" cried Nebuchadnezzar in a passion. "I'll have to bend his stubborn will - yea, I shall do it. I thirst not for his blood; but let the guilty monarch beware how he trifles with my commands! Balphoras! haste thee back with a double guard, and inform Jehoiakim that my orders are not to be trifled with; and moreover, that if he persists in his stubbornness, I shall send sufficient force to drag him into my presence as a guilty culprit."

The communication was in perfect accordance with the desires and expectations of the Chaldean officer. Balphoras was in possession of an amiable mind. He was respectful to his superiors, kind and gentle to his inferiors. Wherever he was known among his countrymen he was greatly beloved. However, he was not insensible to injury or indifferent to abuse. He felt deeply; but had learned to be a greater conqueror than his master, inasmuch as he that governeth his own spirit is greater than he that taketh a city. Balphoras, without being unkind or selfish, desired to witness the humiliation of the King of Judah. The command of his king, therefore, was put in immediate execution, and the Chaldean minister, accompanied by a strong and imposing guard, once more was on his way to demand admission into the presence of the King of Judah.

．　．　．　．　．　．．

"Jared! Well would I have served those guilty dogs, if I had given orders to have their heads taken off. What sayest thou, Jared?"

"They richly deserved it, O king," answered Jared, with his face in another direction, on which played a suppressed smile.

"Let them beware how they insult the King of Judah! Jared! hast thou learned aught of Sherakim's whereabouts?"

"Naught, O king."

"Ungrateful dog! Cowardly fool! Miserable brawler! - Sherakim! Bah! Jared, order more wine. Whom should Jehoiakim fear? Jared! what trouble is there in the porch? Haste thee and see."

Jared hastened to obey the commands of his drunken sovereign, and presently returned.

"The same messenger from the King of the Chaldeans demands an interview with the King of Judah."

"Let him be admitted. Ha! ha! What next?"

Balphoras, with a firm, dignified step, walked into the presence of Jehoiakim, who, in spite of his wine-propped courage, almost trembled beneath the Chaldean's penetrating glance.

"And what hast thou to communicate at this time?"

"My communication is short and decisive."

"The shorter the better - let it be delivered."

"My illustrious sovereign, the King of Babylon, wishes the King of Judah to understand, that his commands are not to be trifled with; and, moreover, that if the King of Judah persists in his stubbornness, he must be dragged into his presence as a guilty culprit."

"Who dares to utter such words in my presence?" cried Jehoiakim, in a rage.

"The Chaldean minister, as the words of his illustrious sovereign."

"Go and tell thine 'illustrious sovereign' that Jehoiakim spits upon his insolent demands."

"Thy raving is in vain. Better far to bridle thy rage and comply. Be it known to the King of Judah, that I have three hundred chosen men of war at my bidding, who wait for the word of command. What is the choice of the King of Judah?"

"Be it known to thee, insolent fool," cried the exasperated king, "that Jehoiakim laughs to scorn thy threats, and spurns thy counsels."

"Alas for thine obstinacy, proud and reckless man!" answered Balphoras, as he left the apartment; "thy doom is sealed!"

After the departure of the Chaldean, Jehoiakim gave orders to his officers to be ready, at all hazards, to defend the royal enclosures against all further intrusion from the Chaldeans.

"A curse upon his guilty head! Ha, ha! 'Dragged into his presence,' eh! Never! Fools! Villains! Let them beware of Jehoiakim's vengeance."

While the King of Judah thus indulged in his wild delirium, a strong detachment of the Chaldean army was on a rapid march towards the royal palace, with orders to make a prisoner of Jehoiakim, and bring him into the presence of the King of Babylon. They soon reached the king's gate, and demanded admittance; which demand was promptly and haughtily refused. This was but the signal for attack, and a furious combat followed. Both the Chaldeans and Jehoiakim's men fought valiantly. The passage was defended with extreme bravery and valor; but after a most desperate struggle, the Chaldeans proved successful in forcing an entrance. The sentry at the palace door was soon overcome, and a company of Chaldeans rushed into the royal mansion; and, after some search, they found the king. Without ceremony he was dragged from his hiding place, and ejected from his palace. A shout of triumph broke from the Chaldeans, which only exasperated their antagonists. Another desperate rush was made for the rescue of their king, but it proved unavailing. He was conducted to the open street amid a general fight. The din of battle brought together vast multitudes, who, seeing their king a captive, added greatly to the strength of Judah's forces; and the Chaldeans found themselves continually attacked from unexpected quarters. Thus the conflict waxed hotter and hotter as the Chaldeans desperately fought their way through the exasperated men of Judah.

Finally, the King of Judah was carried into the presence of Nebuchadnezzar and had he, even then, humbled himself, he might have escaped an awful doom. The behavior of Jehoiakim in the presence of the Chaldean monarch was that of a madman. To every inquiry he replied in the most insulting and abusive epithets; and to seal his own fate he madly rushed on the King of Babylon with his sword, and had it not been that this potentate was on his guard, it would have gone hard with him. This was beyond endurance. Nebuchadnezzar, stung to the quick, grasped his sword, commanded his officers to stand aloof, and faced his enraged foe. They made a few passes, and the sword of the Chaldean was plunged into the heart of the King of Judah."

"Take the ungrateful dog," said the excited Babylonian, "and drag his worthless carcass, and throw it outside the city walls."

The command was immediately put in execution.

Thus perished the wicked king, according to the word of the Lord, by the mouth of his servant Jeremiah.

# CHAPTER VI.

NEBUCHADNEZZAR called together a number of the leading men of Judah and explained his intentions with regard to the government. He also described the killing of Jehoiakim. It was not the policy of the conqueror to establish any rigorous system of public control. He required that Judah should remain as a tributary power, but he desired the country to make progress in its own way, and he took occasion to proclaim that Jeconiah should reign in the place of his father, Jehoiakim, who had just met his fate at the hands of the invader. Those who listened to Nebuchadnezzar were well pleased with his words and also with the elevation of Jeconiah to the throne.

The Babylonian ruler, having now fully accomplished his ends, gave orders for the early departure of the victorious army for the plains of Chaldea. He decided to take with him, as prisoners of war, a number of youths of Judah. He had the twofold object of showing to his people some tangible evidence of his victory and of gaining for his court the advantage of having as aids and attendants some of the more cultured young men of Judea. With the aid of Jeconiah a list of suitable youths was soon prepared by the victorious monarch's officers. These chosen ones were notified, the day of departure was fixed, and all energies were bent toward the speedy return of the army to the land of the Euphrates.

. . . . . ..

Let us now visit some of the homes of Judah, where the mandate of the Babylonian king had fallen as a pall upon the inmates. With one of these homes, located centrally and bearing evidence of prosperity and culture, the reader is already somewhat acquainted. In the room where young Ezrom took leave of his sisters, twenty-five years before, an interesting group had gathered. Monroah, the last survivor of Salome's children, had wedded Amonober, and four lovely children blessed their union. These youths were now orphans, however, the youngest being a maiden of sixteen, who possessed the rare beauty for which the family was noted. Her name was Perreeza. The three brothers were named Hananiah, Mishael and Azariah. The love of these brothers for their sister was returned with all the ardor of an affectionate and sincere girl. These youths were among those selected as prisoners of war.

In company with the young men, when they broke the news of the king's decision to Perreeza, was Jeremiah the Prophet.

"Oh, brothers!" exclaimed the distressed maiden, "must ye be torn away from an only sister? Oh, man of God! What will Perreeza do? My heart will break. Oh, my brothers! We cannot part!" and she fell on the neck of Hananiah and wept bitterly.

"We think it not strange, dear damsel," said the prophet, "that thy young heart is made sad. But the things that are enshrouded in mystery to-day will yet beam forth in wondrous wisdom."

"If to Babylon my brothers go, I must accompany them," said Perreeza, with much decision. "It must be so! Jerusalem will have no charms for me when those I love dearer than life are far away!"

"Surely that would be our joy and desire," replied Azariah, "but alas! I fear it will not be possible to have such a request granted. The exact number is selected and no females are marked on the captive list."

"But dear brother, an effort must be put forth without delay to procure thy sister permission."

"Yea, beloved, and an effort will be put forth, promptly and urgently."

This answer of the brother partly soothed the troubled spirit of the young damsel, and the suggestion on her part opened a little door of hope before the brothers.

Amonober, father of these interesting youths, was a brother of King Josiah. Another brother was Baromon, who had died leaving a widow, Josepha, a son, Daniel, and two daughters. The two families stood among the foremost in the religious and social life of the Holy City. Young Daniel was one of the noble youths chosen by Nebuchadnezzar to go to Babylon. His pious and noble mother and sisters, after their first outburst of grief, committed him to God's care. They became reconciled to their bereavement through the counsel of Jeremiah, who declared that the God of Israel was shaping the whole affair for the advancement of his kingdom on earth.

# CHAPTER VII.

DANIEL and the Amonober children, from their first interview with the officers of the King of Babylon, had left a very favorable impression on the minds of those high dignitaries; and although, in reality, they were but captives of war, they were treated with that high civility due to nobility and rank. This caused much astonishment to the youths themselves, and served in part to calm and reconcile them to their lot. The ardent desire of Perreeza to accompany them to the land of their captivity had been made the subject of their thoughts, and served if possible to deepen in their minds the fountain of pure affection.

Early next morning, the brothers bent their footsteps towards the temporary residence of one of Nebuchadnezzar's officers, with whom, at this time, they had to do. The manner in which they formerly had been received gave them some encouragement to hope that their mission would be crowned with success. They soon reached the "spot, and were admitted.

"And what is the pleasure of these young noblemen of Judah?" asked Barzello, with a pleasant smile.

"Let thy young servants find favor in the sight of their kind and noble master," said Hananiah, "while with deep humility they make known their request. The illustrious Barzello, we trust, will pardon us for this intrusion upon the time of the King of Babylon's noble officer, and listen patiently to their urgent prayer. Thy kind deportment towards thy servants, for these many days, has given them courage thus to stand in thy presence without any painful, distracted fears. We are the sons of Amonober, the brother of King Josiah, under whose reign, for many years, Judah smiled amid peace and plenty. Thy servants were early instructed in the religion of our sainted father, who, with our beloved mother, feared the God of Israel, and worshiped in his holy Temple. While thy servants were yet young, Amonober our father died, and was gathered to his fathers, and today he calmly rests by the side of his illustrious brother, King Josiah. Thus the best of mothers was left a widow with her fatherless children. Thy servants, feeling it no less a pleasure than a duty, endeavored to comply with our father's dying request, by being ever kind to our beloved mother. Thus time passed away for two years, and our pathway once more seemed to be bright and pleasant, when suddenly our mother died. Thy servants were called to stand by the side of her couch before she departed, and these were her parting words:

"'To you, my sons, I commit my sweet Perreeza! Let her youthful feet be tenderly watched by the eyes of love. Whisper words of sweet, brotherly affection in her youthful ears. Oh, deal gently and kindly with the dear, motherless lamb! Remember the dying request of a mother, and throw your arms of protection around your orphan sister.'

"Having concluded these words, our mother closed her eyes, and gave up the ghost. This beloved object of a mother's dying request has been, for many years, the center of thy servants' joy and happiness, and one smile from our own Perreeza will often turn our darkness into day. Our love for her is returned with all the ardor of a sister's pure affection. The sad news of our destined departure from this our native land has well-nigh overwhelmed her heart with sorrow. The thought of parting makes her spirit faint; and thy servants are sincere when they assure their compassionate master that they greatly fear that, if compelled to be separated from her brothers, Perreeza will sink under the deep weight of sorrow, and pass away to the spirit land. In compliance with her very urgent request, thy servants at this time stand as petitioners before their benevolent superior. We are not here to ask to be released from any demand. We patiently yield to the stern necessity that calls us away; but we are here, O most excellent Barzello! to ask a favor for another, which, if granted, will always live in our grateful memories: it is, that Perreeza, our beloved sister, be permitted to accompany us to the land of the Chaldeans."

"And how old is this young sister, of whom ye speak in such terms of commendation?"

"Perreeza has but just commenced her seventeenth year."

"This request must be presented before my lord, the king. Call again at the setting of the sun, and ye shall learn his pleasure in this matter. Be assured that my influence shall be exerted in your behalf."

"And the prayers of thy servants shall always ascend to the God of Judah for ten thousand blessings on the head of Barzello;" and in the most respectful manner, they left the apartment.

. . . . . . .

"Barzello," said the King of Babylon, in a pleasant mood, "are my chosen captives in a ready trim for their departure?"

"All ready at the word of command, O king."

"But what thinkest thou of those brothers? Hast thou had an opportunity of testing their merits?"

"The brothers and cousins, O king, have been repeatedly in my presence, and have given me positive proof that they are youths of very superior abilities and great worth. Their amiable deportment and truly noble bearing have left on my mind a very favorable impression. Indeed, the youths of Babylon, who pride themselves so much on their superior learning and high attainments, might learn precious lessons of wisdom from these very youths of Judah."

"By the gods! Barzello," said the king, laughing heartily, "if at this rate these youths continue to grow upon thy good opinion, before many days thou wilt be a convert to the religion of Judah!"

"Of the religion of Judah I know but little; but if these children are a fair specimen of its operations, I cannot think that there is anything very dangerous or offensive in it."

"Well, when we arrive in Chaldea, we shall give their powers a fair trial. But are there any more brothers in that family?"

"No more, O king," replied the officer, inwardly thanking the king for the question. "There are but three brothers and one young sister."

"She will be a comfort to her mother in the absence of her sons," said the king, in a thoughtful mood.

"But the young damsel has no mother. For many years the children have been both fatherless and motherless."

"Then there must be bitter parting there, Barzello! This young damsel, an only orphan sister, must be bound to her brothers by more than common ties."

"True, O king," answered Barzello, somewhat animated. "The thought of parting grieves them beyond description. It was but this morning that the brothers sought an interview with me on this very point, and pleaded in her behalf with such melting eloquence as well-nigh robbed me of all my generalship. I dismissed them by stating that I would lay their petition before my lord the king, and that I would give them his answer at the setting of the sun."

"Barzello!" said the king, in a firm tone, "I cannot change my purpose in regard to those brothers. Nothing shall prevail upon me to give them up. To Babylon they must go! I have spoken the word! Let there be no pleading in their behalf - I cannot grant their petition."

"I humbly beg my lord the king's forgiveness," replied the officer, with a smile; "but let me assure him that the noble youths have made no petition of that nature." "But what do they ask?" asked the king, with some astonishment.

"They ask, O king, as the greatest favor, that this their young orphan sister, be permitted by the king to accompany her brothers to the land of the Chaldeans."

"And has not this small favor been granted?"

"Barzello now stands in the presence of his sovereign in behalf of the Hebrew damsel, asking for her a permission."

"And the permission is granted. And furthermore, Barzello, see that she is well provided for, and dealt gently with, for the maiden is of kingly line."

"All this shall be strictly attended to, O king," said the well-pleased officer, as he respectfully left the presence of the monarch.

It was now late in the afternoon. The "regent of day" was gradually fading from the sight of the inhabitants of the valley, and was smilingly sinking beyond the western hills, and Barzello hastened his footsteps toward his headquarters. After having reached his apartment, he seated himself, and indulged in some reflections, which, if we might judge from his countenance, we might pronounce to be of a pleasing nature.

While thug musing, he was roused by the entrance of one of his servants.

"What now, Franzo?"

"Three young men and a damsel stand below, desiring the favor of an interview with my master."

"Let them be conducted into my presence; and see thou to it that they receive due respect from all below. They are persons of distinction."

The sister and brothers were conducted into the presence of Barzello, where again they were received with peculiar attention.

"The officer of the king of the Chaldeans is always happy to meet his young friends, and will consider it a great pleasure to add to their comfort and happiness. And this young damsel, I am led to believe, is your sister of whom ye spake this morning."

"This is Perreeza, our sister," replied Azariah; "her sense of obligation to our noble friend for his generous feelings in her behalf, has prompted her to embrace the privilege of appearing in person, to acknowledge her deep gratitude."

"It gives me much pleasure to behold your sister, but I am not aware of any service rendered that calls for a great amount of gratitude."

"Thy servants," said Azariah, "in compliance with the directions received this morning, are in thy presence to learn the will of the king, in regard to thy servants' request, as made known to him through the inter-vention of his generous officer."

"Ye did well to come at the appointed hour. I am always well pleased with strict punctuality. I am happy to inform you, that your request in regard to your sister is very readily granted; and, moreover, the king has given me particular directions to see that she has everything requisite to her perfect comfort in journeying, which directions will be obeyed with the utmost pleasure."

Silent tears of joy coursed down the cheeks of both sister and brothers. They were so affected by the result of their effort, together with the unaffected tenderness of Barzello, that for a short interval they could in no wise give utterance to their feelings. Perreeza was the first to break the spell.

"The most excellent Barzello will please accept the humble thanks of an orphan maiden of Judah, for his kind regards. The God of the fatherless and motherless will surely reward his servant, and cause blessings and prosperity to rest on his household. Thy kindness shall not be forgotten. Our daily prayers shall ascend to the God of Judah in thy behalf, with the smoke of our morning and evening sacrifices."

"And I trust the youthful maiden of Judah," said the officer, in a voice far from being firm, "will live to see many happy years in the fair land of the Chaldeans."

The interview was at an end, and the youths of Judah quietly directed their footsteps to that beautiful mansion which was well known in that vicinity as the "House of Amonober."

# CHAPTER VIII.

ON THE journey to Babylon, nothing of note transpired. The royal captives continued to receive peculiar marks of attention and very clear demonstrations of regard. They readily and justly concluded that all this originated in the generous heart of Barzello; and thus he became more and more endeared to them.

The King of the Chaldeans' return to Babylon, at the head of his victorious army, was hailed with loud acclamations of joy. The great capital of his extensive empire was filled to overflowing with exulting thousands, to welcome the victorious monarch from a brilliant campaign. Proud banners floated in triumph on the high turrets, while a thousand minstrels filled the air with their high-sounding melody.

Nebuchadnezzar was as yet but a young monarch. He spared no pains to render himself acceptable to his people, by a worthy deportment and a liberal encouragement of all improvements throughout his realm, and especially within the city of Babylon. At this period, he was greatly beloved by his subjects, and his popularity was plainly visible in the unbounded welcome with which he was received and escorted to the royal palace.

Erasmus W. Jones

Not far from the king's palace stood a splendid mansion of broad and lofty dimensions. Within the enclosures, everything was arranged with faultless taste. In front, large beds of roses unveiled their charms, and sent forth their sweet fragrance. Each side was well ornamented with shrubbery, and the rear beautified with a garden abundantly filled with delicious fruits. With the permission of the reader, we will now enter. In a richly-furnished apartment within this noble edifice, sat a man of commanding exterior, attired in rich, military official costume. Caressingly on his bosom leaned a young damsel, over whose head sixteen summers might have gently rolled. Joy and gladness beamed in every feature of her lovely countenance.

"Oh, happy day! Father is home again! Jupheena will now be happy. The time of thy absence seemed long and dreary; but thou art back again in our happy home!"

"Yea, my child, I am really home again, and am happy to find my sweet Jupheena as well and as sprightly as ever."

"But my dear father has happily returned sooner than we expected; thy stay in Egypt was but short."

"Short, indeed, my daughter. Pharaoh-Necho, when he saw our powerful legions, soon came to terms of peace; and in this I admire his wisdom. From Egypt, we marched into the capital of Judah, and gained an entrance without resistance.

"My stay in Jerusalem, thou knowest, was but short, and my facilities for observation were not very favorable; but owing to peculiar circumstances, I became partially acquainted with those in Judah who left deep and happy impressions on my mind. I found a few young men of the kingly line, who, in my opinion, were far superior in mind to any I ever had the pleasure of beholding."

"Dear father! that is saying much. Then they must have been very different from their royal relation, of whom thou speakest."

"Thou hast well said, my daughter. Happy would it have been for that distracted nation if one of those youths had graced the throne of Judah, instead of the profligate Jehoiakim."

"Then it appears, surely," said the daughter smilingly, "that true excellence and superiority are not confined to Chaldea. But I hear nothing in praise of Judah's maidens."

"The maidens of Judah are fair - some of them exceedingly fair. Thou wilt wonder, perhaps, to hear that the peculiar grace and artless eloquence of one of these maids of Judah so affected thy father's heart, that he could not refrain from shedding tears."

"And have these interesting captives arrived in the city?"

"Yea, my daughter, they are already in Babylon."

"And shall not thy daughter have the pleasure of seeing this orphan maid of Judah?"

"Yea, verily! this day thou shalt see her; and if thou art

well pleased with her and with her society, she may be an inmate of my house, and a companion for my daughter."

"But can the young maiden converse in Chaldee?"

"She speaks our language, my daughter, with a degree of fluency that is really astonishing. It is evident that her attainments are quite superior, and that all the advantages which Judah's capital could afford have been lavished upon her."

"Oh! it will be delightful to learn beautiful stories of other lands, and have such a sweet and lovely creature for my companion; I am almost impatient to see her."

"I will have her conveyed hither without delay. If I mistake not, the maiden will be delighted to tarry under the roof of one whom she calls her 'bountiful benefactor.' Thy father will now leave for a short season, to attend to some business matters of importance. In two hours I return." And kissing his sweet Jupheena, the soldier hurried out of the apartment. A chariot stood ready at his door, into which he stepped, and was hurried away to another part of the city.

# CHAPTER IX.

THE royal captives, on arriving in the city, were conveyed, according to the strict orders of Barzello, to certain appropriate apartments, prepared for their reception, and nothing requisite to their comfort and entertainment was left wanting. On the very first day of their arrival the God-fearing youths found themselves to be favorites in a land of strangers. The God in whom they trusted gave them adequate strength for their peculiar trials. They found themselves in possession of energy of spirit and courage, that was truly a source of wonderment to themselves. They thought of friends and home with all the fervor of pure affection; but it was not accompanied with those painful, agonizing emotions that are wont to accompany the remembrance of native land and absent friends; in regard to which state of mind they could well adopt the language of one of their happiest monarchs: "This is the Lord's doing, and it is marvelous in our sight."

It was about the ninth hour. The youthful group were seated together.

"Well, cousin," said Azariah, smiling and looking round the apartment, "this has more the appearance of being guests of royalty than poor captives of war."

"Yea, truly," replied Daniel; "and in this we clearly see the loving-kindness of our God, by whom princes rule and kings govern."

"Our kind friend, Barzello," said Hananiah, "has promised to call on us ere the sun sets."

"And he will certainly fulfill his promise," said Mishael.

"We have proved him a genuine and a wise counselor," said Daniel.

"And his loving-kindness shall ever remain deeply graven on our memories," said Azariah.

"Perreeza hopes," said the sister, "that it may be her good providence to be always near the good man, where she may often see his smiling face."

"Our excellent master, under the direction of the King of kings, will order all things for the best," said Hananiah.

"Let us always remember the parting admonitions of our good Prophet," said Mishael, "and calmly submit our all to the wisdom of the Keeper of Israel."

"Even so, amen!" replied the others.

Quick footsteps were heard without. The door opened, and Barzello entered the apartment. The youths unitedly arose, and bowed low, in humble token of respect to the noble officer.

" I trust my young friends from Judah find these

apartments a comfortable resting place."

"Thy servants," replied Daniel, "are overwhelmed with thy kindness, and hope, in some sphere, by a true and honest deportment, to be able to show their benefactor that his kindness is duly appreciated."

"And how does our young maid of Judah feel after her long journey?" asked Barzello, as he smilingly approached Perreeza.

"Thy maid of Judah is in good health; and being so well provided for on her journey, she experienced but a very slight inconvenience."

"But she must be further provided for. She must have a permanent home in the vicinity of her brothers. An officer of the king, in the city, with whom I am well acquainted, having learned something of the history and deportment of this your sister, would desire her, if not contrary to her wishes, to be an inmate of his house, and a companion for his only child - a maiden of sixteen summers. Would this be acceptable to the young damsel?"

"Abundantly acceptable, most kind Barzello!" said Perreeza. "Thy young handmaid is ready at any time to do the pleasure of her protector."

"Then I will accompany thee thither without any delay."

Perreeza withdrew to another apartment, and in a short time, returned, attired in her rich native costume, and giving Barzello a sign that she was ready, they both left the apartment. Soon Perreeza found herself by the side of her kind friend, in a richly-ornamented chariot, that hurried them through the wide and busy thoroughfares. Perreeza was somewhat astonished at the greatness and grandeur of this Gentile metropolis.

"Your Babylon is truly a great city," said she.

"The greatest on record. How in thine eye compares its beauty with the capital of Judah?"

"In the ornamental - in splendid gardens and bubbling fountains - Babylon surely stands far superior."

The chariot halted, and Perreeza found herself in front of one of the most beautiful mansions she had ever beheld.

"And is this the officer's mansion?" asked Perreeza, gazing with a degree of astonishment at the great structure.

"Yea, this is it, fair damsel. But thou appearest somewhat embarrassed. Let the maid of Judah have no fears, for I have every confidence that she will do well."

"Is the noble officer at home?" asked the maid, endeavoring to appear composed.

"He is about the premises, and will soon be in," replied Barzello, with a smile.

"What delicious flowers!" cried Perreeza, breathing a little easier.

"Babylon abounds with the like, fair damsel. But

come, let us enter, for the officer's daughter is in haste
to behold the youthful maid from the land of Judah."

Barzello ascended those steps of spotless marble, and,
with a degree of freedom that seemed to surprise his
young companion, he entered a spacious apartment,
richly furnished and beautifully ornamented, where
Jupheena was ready to receive them, with loving
smiles of welcome.

"Jupheena, this is the young maid from the land of
Judah, of whom thy father spoke," and, directing his
language to Perreeza, at the same time giving Jupheena
a glance that was readily understood, he said, "and,
young damsel, this is the officer's daughter of whom I
spoke."

The two maidens, as if by a magic spell, were drawn to
each other's arms.

"I shall leave you for a short period, Jupheena," said
the officer; "thy father will soon return; when he
comes, thou wilt be most happy to present to him thy
young companion," and Barzello left the apartment,
and thus the two fair ones were left together.

"I am happy to see my young friend from Judah," said
Jupheena. "I have been deeply affected by thy history,
and that of thy noble brothers. I trust, that in the
absence of thy friends, we shall be able to make thee
happy."

"Since we left our beloved Jerusalem, and even before,
we have experienced naught but kindness from the
noble officers of the king, especially the most excellent
Barzello. His sympathies have well-nigh overwhelmed

us, and we shall love him as long as we live, and implore the blessing of the God of Israel to rest upon his household. Was it not he that kindly spoke of thy young handmaiden to thy father?"

"I am not aware who it was that first spoke to my father of the maid of Judah," replied Jupheena, smiling, "but Barzello, surely, is deeply interested in thy welfare."

Barzello again entered, and Perreeza looked for the other officer, but no other officer was present. Jupheena arose, and, taking her young companion by the hand, led her to her father.

"Maid of Judah, I have now the pleasure of presenting thee to my own dear father, the king's officer, under whose roof I trust thou wilt find a welcome home."

"And this is his only daughter, Jupheena, of whom he spoke," said Barzello, highly delighted. "I trust the maid of Judah will find her a pleasant companion."

Such was the effect of this innocent piece of deception on the mind of young Perreeza, that all the response she could make, was to fall on the neck of her young companion, and weep aloud. But those tears were tears of joy; and those lofty walls were witnesses to the fast falling of other tears than those shed by the maid of Judah.

"Blessed be the Lord God of Israel!" cried Perreeza, when partially recovered, "who hath given me favor in the eyes of this people! May Jehovah smile upon his servant Barzello, and upon his lovely daughter, who thus throw open their door to welcome an orphan maid of Israel."

"Thou shalt find under this roof a welcome home," said Barzello, affectionately taking Perreeza by the hand; "in Jupheena thou wilt find a worthy companion and an affectionate friend."

"Thy daughter," answered Jupheena, "will always esteem it a high pleasure to add to the happiness of her young friend."

"And Jehovah assisting me," cried the Hebrew maid, "I will endeavor so to walk before my kind protectors as to be always worthy of their friendly regard."

"If it be pleasing to thy young friend," said Barzello, addressing himself to his daughter, "she may be again conducted to inform her brothers of her new home."

"My brothers will be overjoyed," answered Perreeza, "to learn of the happiness of their sister; and to me, it will afford the greatest pleasure to convey to them the joyful intelligence."

"If it will please my daughter," said Barzello, "she may accompany us. What sayest thou, Jupheena?"

"Thy daughter most gratefully accepts thy kind offer."

"Our young friend, peradventure, will be pleased to see her brothers and cousin without any delay, while Jupheena will accompany her father on an errand of business at the house of an officer nearby. Thou mayest inform thy brothers and cousin that we shall call and see them presently."

Perreeza embraced the opportunity, and, thanking the officer with one of her peculiar smiles, hurried to their apartment.

"Back again, precious Perreeza!" cried Azariah, hastening to meet her. "And did our sister see the king's officer and his young daughter, of whom Barzello spoke?"

"I did!" exclaimed his sister, while unusual joy beamed in her countenance.

"And from thy countenance I am prepared to judge that the interview has been a happy one," said her cousin Daniel.

"Never was there a happier interview, cousin. The noble officer's kindness is unbounded, and his daughter is one of the loveliest beings I ever beheld."

"Perreeza, I trust, will not forget the kindness of Barzello, in the warmth of her gratitude to her new friend," said Azariah.

"Never fear that, my dear brother. The remembrance of Barzello's kindness is too deeply graven on Perreeza's heart to be ever forgotten; and while I remain under the roof of the king's officer, I shall daily become more and more deeply indebted to the kind Barzello."

"It must be that through his kind interposition our beloved sister found so good a home," said Mishael, "and if this officer, under whose roof she has found a shelter, partakes of the spirit of Barzello, her home must be a happy one. Perreeza, does he appear like unto our noble friend?"

"The very image of him!" said the sister, laughing heartily. "Now, brothers and cousin, let Perreeza undeceive you on this point. This noble officer, whose house is to be my future home, is none other than our own illustrious Barzello himself. This truth was made known to me in a way that well-nigh prostrated me. Oh, brothers, is not this delightful?"

"Praised be Jehovah!" broke from the lips of the youths of Judah.

"For conversation we have but a short time," said Perreeza; "Barzello and his lovely Jupheena are below, and will be here in a few moments, and from hence I accompany them to their home. Hark ye! I hear their footsteps."

Barzello, with a smiling countenance, entered the apartment, leading by the hand his beautiful daughter. Perreeza ran to meet her young companion, while the four youths were not wanting in appropriate obeisance to the noble officer; all of which was closely watched by the smiling young Chaldean maid.

"Have our young friends received any communications from any of the king's officers since our last interview?"

"Thy servants have received no communication from any source, since the departure of their kind friend, about the ninth hour," answered Daniel.

"To-morrow morning, peradventure, ye shall learn the pleasure of the king in regard to your future course; and I trust ye will find that our noble monarch is not wholly unmindful of your former rank and station in your own land."

"Permit thy unworthy servants once more," said Azariah, "to acknowledge, with grateful hearts, thy kind regards for their beloved sister, whom thou hast taken as an inmate of thy hospitable mansion. Perreeza will always delight to do thy pleasure, and to be the obedient servant of thy amiable young daughter."

"Your sister, while under my roof, shall not be looked upon in an inferior light. The chosen companion of my daughter will command due respect from those in high circles. The maid of Judah need not feel embarrassed, for her literary attainments will compare favorably with the most polished maidens of her own age in Babylon. She is not a captive. With the noble feeling of a sister's heart, and of her own accord, she accompanied her brothers to a land of strangers. She is as free as any daughter of Chaldea; and therefore my Jupheena will be happy to introduce her to her friends in her real character, as a youthful maid of the royal line of Judah. In thus drawing a line of distinction between yourselves and your sister, far be it from me to think that your present relation to our government renders you, in any real sense, inferior to others - 'tis but a name, and will soon be forgotten; for it is in the power of the king to elevate you, not only to proper citizenship, but to high rank and prominent stations in the government.

"Your sister will now accompany us home. Any article she wishes conveyed thither, shall be sent for without delay. Now, my daughter, are we ready?"

"All ready, father, unless Perreeza has aught unfinished."

"I have naught to hinder," answered Perreeza, with a trembling voice.

Erasmus W. Jones

# CHAPTER X.

IN A ROYAL apartment, decorated in superlative grandeur, sat the powerful monarch of Chaldea. He was alone. His countenance bespoke a degree of self-complacency and satisfaction. Around him, on a rich carpet, were several large scrolls of manuscript, while, in his hand, he held carelessly what appeared to be a well-arranged map of battle fields and grand points of attack. Chaldea, at this time, was the seat of science and learning. Thither the great of other nations resorted to acquire literary distinction. Nebuchadnezzar, from his childhood, had been initiated into all the arts and sciences; and, as he was a youth possessing a superior mind, he made great proficiency in all his numerous studies. Before he ascended the throne, he was pronounced to be one of the brightest scholars within the whole realm; and now, although a monarch, surrounded by a thousand cares and perplexities, he bestowed much thought on his own favorite studies; and one of his most prominent desires was the perpetuity and advancement of learning among his subjects. A dull individual, however high in his rank, could never share the company of the young King of Babylon. All who moved within the royal enclosures, whether as courtiers, under-officers, or domestics, had to be those of discerning minds and intelligence. What exact train of thought occupied the monarch's mind at this time we may better judge, perhaps, from the sequel. He rose from his reclining posture and lightly touched a shining key, which instantly answered in a remote part of the royal palace. The door opened, and an officer bowed himself into the apartment.

"And what is the pleasure of my lord the king?"

"Ashpenaz," said the king, in a familiar voice, "thou knowest well that there is a painful scarcity of waiters to stand in the presence of the king; and even those we have are not what I could desire them to be in point of intelligence and cultivation. This must be remedied without delay. My father's taste in this matter was somewhat different from mine. Far be it from me to cast any reflection on the judgment of my illustrious father; but the glory and splendor of my empire are on the forward march, and things at the royal palace must not be permitted to fall in the rear. I am about to lay a foundation to a measure that will yet shed glory and luster on my reign. What is more mortifying, Ashpenaz, while endeavoring to entertain our own dignitaries, and the visiting nobles of other nations, than to witness the blundering ignorance of our attendants? In this I cast no blame on my worthy and noble officer - by no means.

"In my last campaign I gave orders to convey to Babylon a number of young men of the kingly line, both from Egypt and Judah. From the conversation I had with Barzello, I am led to believe that there are among them some very superior minds. Now, it is the wish of thy king that a number of these youths be taken, and, in company with some of our own young men, be trained up in the knowledge of our arts and sciences, and receive, moreover, particular instruction in all the laws of etiquette, and court customs and maxims, so as to be of efficient service to the king, and at the same time reflect honor on their stations. About their instruction there must be nothing shallow or superficial. There must be thorough work. For this they must have reasonable time. I therefore appoint the period of their studying to be three years, at the end of which let them be brought before the king for examination; and let those who will be able to give satisfaction be permitted to stand before the king. Moreover, as diet of the best sort contributes both to the beauty of the body and the improvement of the mind, let them have their daily portion of the king's meat and the wine which he drinketh. Now, Ashpenaz, for further information thou art to consult Barzello. He will select a certain number of young men, and deliver them over to thee, and thou art to lose no time in placing them under suitable instructors."

"Thy servant," replied Ashpenaz, "is ever happy to obey the orders of his illustrious sovereign, which are always issued in that profound wisdom derived only from the gods."

This officer stood high in the estimation of the king. He was calm, dignified, and deeply experienced in all things pertaining to the duties of his office. For a long time he had served as a confidential servant of the king's father, and was highly honored by young and old at the court. This dignitary was soon on his way towards the house of his friend Barzello.

"Good-morning to my friend Ashpenaz," said Barzello, with a welcome smile.

"And a good-morning to our excellent Barzello," was the hearty response.

"And how do things move on at the palace?"

"Oh, pleasantly. Our young monarch is bent on thorough reform in all deficient quarters."

"Babylon needs reforming; and may he never pause until the work is perfected. Long life to our good monarch!"

"Ah! my good Barzello, if all that is to be accomplished, he needs a long life indeed. But I have but a short time to tarry. The king desires a number of the royal captives of Judah and Egypt to be placed under proper instructions to prepare them, after three years' training, to be royal waiters at the palace. In thy wisdom thou art to select from among them the most perfect in body and mind, and deliver them over to my charge; and, according to the orders of his majesty, I shall immediately place them under suitable teachers."

"This will be attended to without delay," answered Barzello. "Of those from Egypt, there are quite a number of youths of high origin, and who, for aught I know, may possess superior powers of mind. I have had no great facilities to test their capacities. Of those from Judah, there are only four that I can with confidence recommend to the care and charge of my worthy friend. These four are noble specimens of humanity - beautiful in bodily form and complexion, and truly amiable and excellent in mind. I will assure my worthy friend that, of all the acquaintances I ever formed among men, and they have been quite numerous in different lands, none ever impressed me so favorably as these four youths from the land of Judah. They worship no god but the God of the Hebrews. In this they show but their faithfulness and their consistency. My worthy friend will pardon my warmth in speaking of these children, for there are incidents connected with their history, which I need not now mention, that have greatly endeared them to thine unworthy friend; and I have no doubt that thou wilt find them to be all they are recommended to be."

"I have all confidence in the judgment and wisdom of my worthy friend," answered Ashpenaz, "and it affords me much pleasure to hear such a favorable report of those who are to be placed under my charge; and I assure my good Barzello, that their worth and excellence will be duly noticed and appreciated."

"If thou art in haste, I will accompany thee without delay to the young men's apartments; perhaps thou wouldst be pleased to see them."

"After such a warm recommendation, it will certainly be quite a favor - but where is thy sweet Jupheena? This call will hardly recompense me, if I must leave without a glance at that little beauty."

"Ah, indeed! Perhaps our good friend Ashpenaz will have no objection to gaze on two beauties instead of one."

"All the better, my friend."

A female servant was sent to the young ladies' room to inform them that they were wanted below, and in a few minutes the two girls were seen, side by side, marching into the presence of the delighted officers. Perreeza never appeared lovelier. Attired in the rich, flowing simplicity of her Hebrew costume, with a degree of blushing modesty on her yet animated countenance, she appeared almost angelic. Jupheena, perfectly acquainted with her father's friend, felt not the least embarrassment.

"Two beauties instead of one, surely," said Ashpenaz, gazing with wonder on the fair form of Perreeza.

Barzello took the maid of Judah by the hand, and, approaching his friend, said:

"This is young Perreeza, of the royal line of Judah, who, of her own accord, accompanied her brothers to the land of the Chaldeans, and has seen fit to favor us with her company."

"No very small favor, Barzello," cried Ashpenaz, bowing low. "I hope the partiality of the gods will not make us quarrel."

"Let not my noble friend be unjust to the gods. If the maid of Judah is an inmate of the house of Barzello, I trust that three brothers and a cousin, given to the sole charge of Ashpenaz, will convince him that the gods are not partial."

"Ah! that will do," said Ashpenaz, still gazing on the maid of Judah.

"Perreeza," said Barzello, "from pure love for her three brothers, of whom I spake, saw fit to leave her native land and venture her future destiny among strangers."

"I trust," answered Ashpenaz, "they are indeed worthy of such a sister's pure affection."

"That is a point soon settled in the minds of all who

have the pleasure of their acquaintance."

"Permit me to congratulate my young friend, Jupheena, on the happy addition to the number of her youthful friends."

"Our beloved Ashpenaz may well congratulate," replied the young beauty; "and let him be assured that his congratulations are warmly appreciated."

"And how does our young friend from Judah enjoy the society of her Chaldean friends?"

"Thy young handmaiden enjoys their society much," modestly replied Perreeza. "If she stands in any danger, it must be from an excess of kindness."

"I trust the maid of Judah will sustain no material injury from any amount of kindness received in my house," said Barzello, laughing. "If she does, she must charge it to herself; for, under the circumstances, to be less kind is entirely out of our power."

"Barzello," cried the visitor, "thy house is a famous spot for officers to forget their great hurry. Come, my good friend, business is pressing; let us be away. A good-day to the 'two beauties instead of one.'"

And the two officers hurried from the apartment, entered a chariot, and were on their way to the appointed place.

"A charming damsel that, Barzello."

"All of that, my worthy friend."

"What are her literary attainments?"

"All that Judah's capital could bestow."

"How will she compare with the refined maids of Babylon?"

"She will compare favorably with the most polished in Chaldea."

"Verily. And the brothers?"

"All thy richest fancies could paint them."

"And yet captives of war!"

"Yea - captives of war."

"The captivity of genius must be of short duration."

The chariot halted. The two officers alighted, and without delay they hastened to the apartments of the Hebrew youths.

"A happy day to the youths of Judah," said Barzello, in a lively tone. "This is my noble friend, Ashpenaz, a high officer of the king at the palace. From this hour ye are to be under his special directions."

"Thy servants," replied Daniel, bowing gracefully, "will be greatly delighted to be placed in any spot where they can be of service to their worthy superiors."

"To-morrow, then," said Ashpenaz, "ye shall enter upon new duties, and commence your important studies. Your teachers are in readiness - men of superior powers of mind, and well versed in the art of teaching. The king himself will be greatly interested in your progress, and therefore has prepared apartments for the students within the royal enclosures, where he will at times appear personally to learn of their advancement. To-morrow, at the third hour, ye will hold yourselves in readiness to be conveyed thither."

"Thy servants will be in readiness at the appointed hour," said Daniel.

"Now for the Egyptians, Barzello," said Ashpenaz, smiling, as they left the apartment.

# CHAPTER XI.

AT THE appointed hour, our youths, in company with many others, were conveyed to their new habitation, which was a beautiful building, erected in the vicinity of the king's palace. Here all the students were received with great civility, and commended to their different apartments. The four Hebrews were not separated, but were permitted to remain as heretofore. They found that everything conducive to their comfort and enjoyment had been provided here as well as at the apartments they had left. Hitherto they had no knowledge of the manner in which they were to receive instruction, or the precise nature of their studies. They knew the Chaldeans to be noted for their learning, and they were not without their fears lest the Babylonian youths who were to be their fellow-students should outstrip them, and leave them far in the distance; however, they were fully determined to acquit themselves to the utmost of their ability, and leave the result with the God of their fathers. Nothing could have given them greater satisfaction than the course marked out for them by the king. Indeed, if it had been left to their own choice to select, it could not have been otherwise. From the days of their early childhood they had been close students, and they had become well versed in Hebrew lore, and had a fair knowledge of Chaldee, which was often studied in Judah, as an ornamental branch of education. This proved a very favorable item in their experience, but there were numerous studies before them, to which, as Jews, they were utter strangers, and to acquire even a respectable knowledge of which demanded much time and perseverance. The king was aware of this when he appointed the time of their probation to be three years. The Egyptian youths were of royal descent, and had some knowledge of the Chaldee, and were well acquainted with several branches of learning pertaining to their native land. The Chaldean portion of the students were mostly of the city of Babylon, and already somewhat advanced in what was considered the higher branches.

When conducted to their respective rooms, they were given to understand that, at a certain signal, they were all to assemble below, where Ashpenaz would meet them, address them, and enlighten them in regard to the duties of their future course.

The four Hebrews were quietly seated in one of their apartments, each one engaged in satisfying his curiosity by gazing at the richly carved casings and highly ornamented articles of furniture.

"Well, cousins," said Daniel, with a smile, "I trust they will not un-Hebrew us with their Chaldean mysteries."

"If I forget thee, O Jerusalem!" said Azariah, with feeling, "let my right hand forget her cunning."

"Let my tongue be palsied if I forget, for a day, the loved ones at home," said Hananiah.

"When the sweet memories of our beloved Prophet shall be obliterated from this bosom," said Mishael, laying his hand upon his breast, "then let me be utterly forsaken."

"The law of Jehovah shall be the rule of our actions," said Daniel; "to him we yield our hearty and willing obedience."

The grand signal was heard below, and, without delay, the young men, from different parts of the building, were seen hurrying to the commodious apartment set apart for the occasion. Here they found a number of the king's officers assembled, among whom the youths of Judah recognized the pleasant countenance of Barzello. They were soon seated in perfect order, and Babylon never witnessed, in personal appearance, a more interesting group of youths. They were received by the officers with a smile of satisfaction, and with a look of admiration. Presently, the dignified form of Ashpenaz was seen moving slowly towards the rostrum; he ascended, gracefully bowed to the officers on either side, and proceeded:

"It is of the utmost importance that those who are destined to minister in the king's presence should be well initiated into the ways and manners, maxims and customs of our nation, and be well versed in all the learning of the Chaldeans. Nothing short of this can meet the demands and reasonable expectations of our great monarch; and for this he has carefully provided every facility. Your teachers are of the most superior in the realm, and an ample period is appointed for the perfection of your accomplishments.

"In addition to literary attainments, the king looks for moral integrity, uprightness of character, and true amiability of deportment. Without these, the most learned can never add to the real dignity of the court, nor to the stability of the Empire; but, on the contrary, such a one destitute of moral principle must prove a dangerous element in any and all communities. Let this be deeply impressed on your youthful minds, and seek earnestly to cultivate those nobler powers of the mind, as well as the intellectual faculties.

"Those of you from Egypt, and especially those of you from Judah, have no faith in our gods, or sympathy with our mode of worship. From your infancy ye have been taught to do homage to the God of your fathers and to his worship ye have pledged your future lives. The King of Babylon, in his great wisdom, has seen fit to put no obstacles between you and the worship of your deities. Ye are at liberty to serve your gods and adore after the dictates of your own consciences; and, moreover, ye are not required to perform any act that may be contrary to your religious convictions. I trust that this great favor will be rightly appreciated, and never abused. While ye are thus kindly permitted to worship your own gods, show no disrespect to those who may differ from you, and on whose good-will and favor your future success must greatly depend.

"As a proof of his high regard for your physical and intellectual prosperity, the king has appointed your meat and drink to be conveyed from his own table. This, indeed, is an honor conferred on but few in Babylon. Thus, ye readily perceive that nothing is wanting that is in the least calculated to enhance your comfort or speed your literary progress. Ye have but to apply yourselves diligently to your studies and be careful to maintain a correct deportment, and ye shall reap the reward of fidelity, in being permitted to stand in the presence of the king.

"It is the desire of your sovereign that those from Egypt and Judah be known hereafter by names more suitable to the country in which ye now abide. These names ye shall hereafter learn from your teachers. Ye may now return in perfect order to your respective apartments. To-morrow at the second hour, at a given signal, ye will appear at this place again, and formally enter upon your studies."

The four youths, after having reached their rooms, for a while sat in silence; and from the countenance of Daniel it might have been easily gathered that all was not well. The brothers were not slow to notice this, and it caused them some uneasiness. Usually their cousin took the lead in all conversation, but at this time Daniel was mute.

"Well, cousin," said Azariah, "how wast thou pleased with the address of our new master?"

"Highly pleased, upon the whole. He surely is a man of kind feelings and refined taste."

"But my dear cousin seems somewhat disconsolate and much less cheerful than when we left this apartment one hour ago. We are at a loss to find a cause for this sudden change."

"I perceive that a certain part of the address, which struck me as rather unfortunate for us, was not looked upon in that light by my worthy cousins."

"I suppose thou hast reference to that part relating to the change of names. For my part, I am not over-tenacious on that point, for to me thou wilt always remain 'Cousin Daniel,' and to thee, I trust, I shall always be 'Cousin Azariah;' and if the Chaldeans prefer to call me Bel-sha-bo-raze-ba-phoo, and my Cousin Daniel Sha-go-mer-zalta-ba-phee, or some other long name, let them by all means be gratified."

"My worthy cousin is mistaken in regard to this point," said Daniel, smiling, while the three brothers, for the first time in Babylon, joined in a hearty laugh. "As far as names are concerned, they are welcome to add on the syllables to their hearts' content; but, seriously, cousins, there is a point that, if not rightly managed, will entangle us in serious difficulties. I have reference to that part which made mention of our meat and drink. How can we, as Hebrews, defile ourselves with meats, portions of which are offered to idols, and with wine sacrificed to the gods of Chaldea? This would be in direct violation of the law of our God. To this we can never consent; and, moreover, we are not accustomed to these dainties, and such high living can never be conducive to our health and happiness. Ye know, cousins, that from beholding the drunken degradation of those in high authority in Judah, our parents, many years ago, arrived at the wise conclusion that their children, in order to escape the pit-falls into which others had fallen, should never be counted among wine-drinkers. To this desire of our fond parents we strictly adhered while in Jerusalem, although often ridiculed by drunken wit, and frowned upon by countenances flushed with strong drink. Shall we, then, in a strange land, forget the covenant of our God, and violate our sacred obligations to our beloved parents? No, cousins, this must never be. I trust we may yet be excused, for we were informed that we would not be required to perform any act against our religious convictions. Our food must remain simple, as in Judah; and by this we shall not only adhere to the requirements of Jehovah, but we shall also be better able to master those arduous studies which stand before us in such formidable array."

"Right, noble cousin," cried Azariah, hastening up to Daniel and grasping him affectionately by the hand; "always right! On thee be the sole management of the business; and we are confident that, as usual, under the blessing of our God, we shall come forth triumphantly."

"First of all, then, I must have an interview with our kind master."

Footsteps were now heard approaching their apartment. Daniel opened the door, and, finding there a servant of Ashpenaz, addressed him:

"Will the servant of our noble master have the kindness to convey to him a message, in few words, from one of the youths of Judah?"

"The servant of my lord Ashpenaz will always be happy to do all in his power for the comfort and happiness of those from Judah; and any message to my lord I am ready to convey."

"The message is this: Daniel, of the captivity of Judah, asks the favor of a short interview with his kind lord, Ashpenaz."

The servant respectfully bowed and departed, and, in a few moments, Daniel stood in the presence of his kind friend.

" And what is the pleasure of my young friend

from Judah?"

Here Daniel explained, in an eloquent manner, the objections he and his three companions had to partaking of the portion of the king's meat and the wine which he drank.

"This is rather a delicate point, my young friend," answered Ashpenaz, with a degree of perplexity visible on his countenance. "If your meat and drink were of my own appointment, your request could be granted with the greatest ease and pleasure; but since the order comes from the king, I see not how it can be granted without disobedience to superior orders. The king desires to give you every opportunity to improve, if possible, your appearance. I fear my lord the king. For why should he see your faces worse looking than the children which are of your degree? Then shall ye make me endanger my head to the king."

"Prove thy servants, I beseech thee, ten days," said Daniel, turning towards Melzar, "and let them give us vegetable food, and pure cold water to drink. Then let our countenances be looked upon before thee, and the countenances of the children that eat of the portion of the king's meat; and as thou seest, deal with thy servants."

"Well," replied Ashpenaz, smiling, "if the king's object is accomplished, I trust he is not tenacious about the article of food; so, Melzar, let our young friends be gratified in this respect. Let them have a trial of ten days, and, if at the end of that time they have retained their beauty and freshness, let them be fed with vegetables."

"Permit me, in the absence of my three cousins, to offer their gratitude, with my own, to our noble lord for his kind favor," said Daniel, gracefully bowing himself out of the apartment.

The morning of the tenth day dawned upon our Hebrew captives. Their days of trial were soon over, and they felt no fear of the scrutinizing gaze of Melzar. Health and beauty played on their fair cheeks, and they were well prepared for the inspection; and Melzar declared, with due humility, in their presence, that such countenances were not to be found in all Babylon. Now, Melzar was an excellent judge of beauty.

Thus Melzar took away the portion of their meat, and the wine that they should drink, and gave them pulse.

# CHAPTER XII.

AS BOTH Barzello and his daughter were highly esteemed in Babylon, Perreeza made many delightful acquaintances and was much sought after. She was happy in her new life, and by her many accomplishments and sweet disposition greatly endeared herself to her new found friends.

Among the acquaintances of Barzello, with whom the king's trusted officer had been on terms of intimacy for a long term of years, was one Joram, a rich merchant of the city. Joram was understood to have great influence at court, owing to the fact that he had traveled all over the then known world and possessed a valuable knowledge of many nations. His life was a mysterious one, and, while he was credited with being the richest man in Babylon, he was little seen outside of his place of business; but many politicians consulted him, and the king had been known to send his chariot for Joram day after day when great affairs of state were on hand. It had also leaked out that people of distinction from other countries visited the great merchant, and it was correctly surmised in political circles that Joram had helped to shape many a commercial treaty in the interests of the Babylonian monarch.

With all his mystery and reticence and secret power,

Joram was a loyal subject of Nebuchadnezzar and ably seconded the king's efforts for advancing the greatness of Babylon. His family consisted of his wife and an adopted son. The latter was a young man of fine attainments, and was being educated in statecraft as well as mercantile affairs.

Early one evening Barzello had succeeded in persuading Joram to accompany him home. He had spoken of the young captives and the beautiful Perreeza, and wished the merchant and his family to know them. The two elderly men were accompanied to the officer's house by Mathias, the adopted son of Joram. They were warmly greeted by Jupheena, who smilingly conducted Mathias to another part of the house for the purpose of introducing him to Perreeza.

"Maid of Judah," said Jupheena, "I have the pleasure of presenting thee to the honorable Mathias, son of our most excellent Joram."

At these words the maid arose with calmness and beautiful dignity, appearing like an angel in human form, and gently responded to the very low bow of the young Babylonian. The conversation soon became animated. Mathias talked with all the warmth of his noble nature, producing a very favorable impression on the mind of the maid of Judah.

"To me it is quite refreshing," said Perreeza, "to hear a name that is familiar in Israel. I have many relatives in Judah who are called by thy name."

"Our national feelings are strong," said the young man, "and, if I have learned correctly, this feeling is said to be stronger in the Hebrew heart than in all others."

"I am not so well prepared to vouch for the correctness of the sentiment," said Perreeza, "but if my own feelings be an index to the sentiments of others of my nation, the saying is abundantly true."

"It is certainly an admirable trait of character," said the young man, "and the individual in a foreign land who can think of the home of his fathers without strong emotion is not, in my opinion, an individual to be envied."

"Permit the maid of Judah to thank her friend for that noble sentiment."

Here the conversation was arrested by a signal from Barzello, and the young people went forward to join the other members of the family.

"This is Perreeza, of the royal line of Judah," said Barzello, taking the maid gently by the hand, "whom I have the great pleasure of presenting to my illustrious friend Joram."

The blushing maid modestly bowed while Joram took her by the hand and said, with unusual feeling, "May the blessing of the God of thy fathers, dear maid, accompany thy footsteps in a foreign land."

This blessing from the lips of a Babylonian was deeply appreciated by the young woman, who was already touched by the kindness with which she was met on every hand.

"The Lily of the Valley," said Joram, referring to Jupheena, "has found a sweet companion, and the maid of Judah, I trust, will not be displeased if, by the request of my good friend Barzello, I give her the name of an appropriate rose."

"On the contrary," said Perreeza, "thy young hand-maiden is very grateful to the noble friend of Barzello for every token of his notice and kind regard."

"Then, maid of Judah," said Joram, "thy floral name, from this hour, is the Rose of Sharon."

"The Rose of Sharon!" cried Jupheena. "Oh, Perreeza, is not that delightful? Rose of Sharon!"

"Beautiful, indeed!" said Perreeza, "and better than all, it is the sweet rose of my own native land."

"True, young maid, true," said Joram, "'tis the favorite rose of Judah."

"The noble friend of Barzello will accept the thanks of his unworthy young acquaintance for his very happy compliment," said Perreeza.

"Well," responded Joram, "one Hebrew lay, accompanied by the harp of Judah, will recompense us a thousand times."

"That shall be attended to with pleasure," said Perreeza, and the two young women left to bring the harp.

"Now, my good friend, what thinkest thou of the maid of Judah?" asked Barzello.

"The Rose of Sharon is all loveliness," said Joram. "Ah, my friend, sawest thou not the majestic glance of that dark eye, the inimitable hue of those fair cheeks, the full perfection of those lips, the glossy richness of the profuse curls, and the marble whiteness of that model neck? Add to this, my friend, the amiability of her character and her ripe accomplishments, and in her we find a charming and suitable companion for the daughter of Barzello."

"Joram, are the Hebrew women noted for their beauty?"

"Perhaps no nation can boast of greater fairness of complexion among their females than the Jews."

"Now the youthful maid of the royal line of Judah will make us happy with one of her Hebrew melodies, she having brought her favorite harp," said Barzello.

"My kind friend may well say favorite harp," replied Perreeza, with deep emotion; "for to me, surely, it is a very precious treasure. For many years it has been in our family. To me it was left by the dearest of mothers, and to her it was given by a brother beloved, who found an early grave."

This was received by the company in silence, but it was noticed that Joram was deeply affected.

Perreeza took the instrument in her arms, swept her delicate hand over the well-tuned strings, and, after a moment's pause sang in seraphic tones a plaintive melody peculiar to her life in Jerusalem.

Profound silence fell on the assembly after her song was finished. The performance and its effect were such that applause or compliments would have sounded ill-timed. All gazed with solemn delight on Perreeza as she laid aside her harp and took her seat beside Jupheena.

Suddenly, the disappearance of Joram was noticed, and Barzello sprang up in an agitated manner. The merchant was not in the room, and none had seen him depart.

"In the name of the gods, what has befallen my good friend!" cried the officer, as he went to the adjoining apartment.

"Be calm," faintly replied the voice of Joram, as the host came to where he was reclining.

"Barzello," said the guest, "thou hast given me reason these many years to believe in thy friendship."

"Thou art not in the least mistaken," responded Barzello.

"Then I shall proceed without delay to explain my singular conduct, and, in making these developments, I am confident I shall share the sympathies of my kind friend. To-night my heart has been almost rent with contending emotions. I have been well-nigh over-whelmed with both sadness and joy. During my long residence in this part of the world a degree of mystery has hung over myself and family, and even to-day my country and origin are not known. For many years past I have had strong doubts in regard to the wisdom of this course of secrecy. The time has at last arrived when my life history must be divulged.

"In the first place, then, let me inform you that I am a

Hebrew. I was born of noble and wealthy parents who lived within the metropolis of Judah. I was the pride of my father, and by my mother I was almost idolized. Being of a lively temperament I was fond of company and overfond of amusements. I was sent to one of the city's leading halls of learning and found but little trouble in mastering my studies. I was early thrown into the companionship of those who had not the fear of God before their eyes. I drank in their spirit, and, consequently, the yoke of parental authority became painful to my youthful neck. My affection for parents and near relatives was strong, and it was not without a hard struggle that I yielded to the enticements of older transgressors. Gradually I became the willing companion of youths whose chief object was amusement.

"One night we tarried together until a late hour and several of my companions indulged freely in wine. Before we left the scene of our carousal they had become quite boisterous. I was more sedate than usual, though entering into the spirit of the occasion. At that late hour the watchmen, or guards, of the city found it necessary to interfere and check our hilarity. A fight ensued in which I took part. Being recognized by one of the officers, I fled the city rather than face the disgrace of trial and punishment. Taking leave of my sisters, I was soon far from the land of my birth. My last act was to present to my favorite sister the harp which thou hast seen and heard to-night.

"My dear friend, judge of my surprise and joy when I recognized in the maid of Judah one of my own relatives. The beautiful and noble orphan who is your daughter's companion in this house is none other than my own niece.

"I feel that my long neglect of my surviving relatives makes me unworthy even to serve them, but I am determined now that this sweet damsel shall share in my wealth and enjoy all the advantages which my efforts can obtain for her, together with her worthy brothers. In this way I can make partial atonement for the mistakes of the past."

This remarkable revelation was soon made known to the excited company. With a cry of joy the fair maid of Judah fell into the arms of her uncle. Tears fell from every eye. The "Lily of the Valley" wept, and so did the brave soldier, her father, and so did young Mathias. The scene was one that pen cannot adequately describe, but happiness was supreme in the household.

# CHAPTER XIII.

AT THE school, agreeable to the expectations of Barzello, the four Hebrews made astonishing progress in their multiform studies. Those profound sciences which had cost their teachers years of ceaseless toil were, by these four young men, mastered with apparent ease. They soon became objects of wonder to their instructors, and were pronounced favorites of the gods. Ashpenaz often would have an interview with them, and soon they became the objects, not only of his admiration, but also of his friendship. This became visible to their fellow-students, and jealousy, accompanied by malice, found a ready entrance to more than one heart. Alas, for poor fallen humanity!

Among the students from the city of Babylon there were two young men, brothers, whose father, by a sudden freak of fortune, had arrived at the possession of much wealth. For some years these young men's advantages had been quite favorable, and withal they had not been negligent in their studies. They were exceedingly vain of their acquirements, and their pride and arrogance kept pace with their vanity. The success of others, to them, was invariably a source of mortification.

They had already heard complimentary reports of the youths of Judah from no mean sources; and they became their foes, and were determined to see them humbled. As students, they met but seldom, and the real acquirements of the Israelitish youths were not known to these envious Chaldeans. With these two victims of vanity and envy was cast the unhappy lot of another youth, their cousin. He was of "humbler birth," as the term is used, but almost infinitely their superior in everything that beautifies and adorns humanity. He was frank, generous, noble, and endowed with no small share of natural wit. For his conceited cousins he was anything but a pleasant companion; and daily was their arrogance rebuked by his far-searching repartees. Thus have we introduced to the reader three young Chaldeans, Scribbo and Shagoth, with their Cousin Apgomer.

"I cannot, for my part," said Scribbo, "see the propriety of elevating these contemptible captives to share equal privileges with the native sons of Chaldea. Surely the king, in this, has betrayed a lamentable lack of discernment."

"Truly!" replied Shagoth, with an air of consequence. "And if he does not ere long see his folly, and retrace his steps, he will lose my confidence, and that of all the members of our house."

"May the gods pity the king!" cried Apgomer, with a feigned solemn visage. "Peradventure, that in the great pressure of business he forgot that the confidence of my illustrious cousins was so essential to his well-being, as well as the safety and perpetuity of the empire."

"My remarks were called forth by the sensible statement of my brother," said Shagoth, peevishly;

"and it would have been perfectly excusable in thee to have remained silent, until I should have thought fit to make some remarks suitable to the capacity of thy mind."

"My worthy cousin will, I trust, in the plenitude of his overflowing generosity, pardon the officiousness of his unworthy servant of limited capacities, and believe him when he assures thee that those remarks were offered as an humble apology for the great sovereign of the Chaldean empire; and I still hope that, in the richness of thy clemency, thou wilt forgive him."

"I trust," replied Scribbo, "we are able to appreciate thy remarks, and undoubtedly they will receive the respect they deserve. If thou couldst have thy quarters removed to the society of these pretending foreigners, methinks it would better suit thy groveling taste."

"Such a sudden bereavement might be more than my tender-hearted cousins could well endure. May the gods forbid that I should be the means of over-whelming you with unnecessary sorrow! And, besides, I fear I am not such a favorite of the gods as to receive such a marked favor."

"A prodigious favor to be the companions of illiterate captives!" cried Scribbo, with a disdainful curl of his lip. "The Chaldean who calls that a favor, is anything but an ornament to his country."

"We may have different tastes in regard to ornament," replied the good-natured cousin, looking with an arch smile on his cousin's heavy and useless jewelry. "As for me, I am a plain young man. I value the useful far above the ornamental. I consider healthy ablutions and clean linens far more desirable than the decoration of our persons with ornamental trash. And why may it not be so in the government? So much in regard to ornaments. 'Ignorant and illiterate captives.' Ah, cousin! Believest thou this? Dost thou not rather hope that this is so? Hope on! The day of trial hastens apace! Hope vigorously and diligently; for such hope is of short duration. Ye expect, by your superior learning, to humble the youths of Judah in the presence of the king and his nobles. Ye are sanguine in your expectations. Already ye see their heads bowing with shame and embarrassment, while your own brows are decorated with well-earned laurels. Do ye not already enjoy the bliss of the prophetic vision, until the bursting in of the reality? Ah, ye do! Now think it not over-officious in your cousin of low capacity to assure you that your hopes are but the baseless fabrics of vain minds. The day of examination will reveal to your astonished sensibilities that ye have dreamed the dream of fools. Those noble young men, who are the objects of your hatred, will soar above you triumphantly, and their enemies will be covered over with shame. Let me give you fair warning! Ye are ignorant of the strength of those youths, over whom your vain imaginations appear to triumph with such ease."

"Our forbearance, brother, I fear, only encourages the insolence of this, our ungrateful relative," said Shagoth, in anger. "How soon these upstarts forget their poverty when they are permitted to mingle in good society."

"And how soon they forget the kind hands that lifted them up from their low estate!" answered Scribbo, casting a reproachful glance in the direction of Apgomer.

"Now, cousins," said Apgomer, smilingly, "since these charges are thrown out against me, without going through the usual form of asking permission, I shall at once take the liberty of repelling them.

"In the first place, I am charged with being an 'upstart,' and of too soon forgetting my poverty. This I deny. I have, by no means, forgotten my own poverty, or the low condition of my ancestors. Let us look at this for a moment. Painful as it may be, I believe ye do occasionally admit that I am your cousin. Well, then, be it remembered that I am your cousin. Our fathers were brothers, and our grandfather was one and the same person. It is well known to you that our respected grand-sire was an individual who had to plod his way along through the very steeps of poverty, and procure a little bread for his family by humble employments. In poverty he lived, and in deep poverty he would have died, had it not been for the grateful regard of one of his sons; of the other, I have nothing to say at present. Now to some, who have suddenly risen from poverty to a degree of affluence, it proves a source of deep mortification to remember that they sprang from a low origin. But is this the case with your cousin Apgomer? Have I forgotten the source whence I sprang? Does it create a blush on this cheek to remember that my grandfather was poor, and that my father had to win his bread through the sweat of his brow? Whoever has forgotten the poverty of his father and grandfather, be it known that Apgomer is not that youth.

"So much in regard to the first charge. Now for the second. I am accused of forgetting those 'kind friends, who lifted me up from my low estate.' Those friendly hands who helped me to the situation I now hold are, by no means, forgotten; they are deeply graven upon a grateful memory. While this pulse shall beat, and while this heart shall throb, the names of Barzello and Joram will, by me, be fondly cherished. Then there was much opposition from certain quarters. There were those who could not discern the propriety of my being elevated to an equality with those of greater wealth; and I am not sure, since the king has not seen fit to retrace his steps, but that he has lost the confidence of those concerned. Cousins! I am ever grateful to those kind friends who so nobly took me by the hand. I know well who they are, and I know well who they are not."

"Surely our young instructor is becoming eloquent," said Scribbo, rather crestfallen.

"Yea, verily," replied his brother; "and who can withstand such a mighty torrent of oratory? Let us away to the groves!" And Apgomer was left, for the time being, the sole occupant of the apartment.

# CHAPTER XIV.

DAYS, weeks, months, and years, have passed away, and the great day of examination has arrived - that day for which that youthful group has looked so long, with mingled feelings of pleasure and embarrassment. This day broke on the capital of Chaldea with unusual brightness. The sun shone brightly in a cloudless firmament, and Nature had put on her sweetest smile. In the vicinity of the king's palace it was evident that something of more than ordinary interest was that day to be attended to. Officers hurried to and fro. Dignitaries bowed to one another with additional smiles. Groups of citizens of the better class appeared here and there, in earnest conversation. Magnificent chariots, drawn by fiery steeds, halted at the king's gate about the third hour. A splendid national flag proudly waved on the high pinnacle of the students' building, while each window presented ingenious mottoes appropriate for the occasion.

The place appointed by the king for the public examination of the students, was a magnificent audience room that stood within the royal grounds, and in close proximity to the palace. This apartment was finished in the highest perfection of art, and, in addition, on this occasion, was decorated with ornaments suitable for the day.

At an early stage, the room was well filled with the first of Babylon's aristocracy, together with some few who had no just claim to title. Appropriate seats were reserved for the king and his attendants, who were soon expected to make their appearance. Among the number assembled there were many of the students' parents. With but two or three exceptions, joy and good feeling appeared to be the expression of every countenance, while, with hearts free from envy and malice, they gazed on the comely forms of those before them. Among these smiling countenances might have been seen three individuals - a father, mother and daughter - who smiled, indeed, but whose smiles would never have convinced the beholder that they were an index to noble and generous hearts.

"'Twas a strange notion of the king, surely," said the daughter, "to bring these Hebrew captives in competition with the refined minds of Chaldea; I cannot account for it, unless it is purposely done to show them their great inferiority, and thus, by to-day's exercises, teach them a lesson of humility that they will not soon forget; for no one can be so unwise as to think that such illiterate foreigners can appear to any advantage in a place like this."

"Thy remarks, daughter, are perfectly correct," answered the mother. "I am at a loss, myself, to understand the king in this. But thy brother, Shagoth, has learned, of late, that these Jews are far from being dull scholars; and he fears that, by some strange contrivance, they have worked themselves into the graces of Ashpenaz. I have my fears that these reports are too true. Yet I have strong hopes that in this trial of learning, they will fall entirely below thy accomplished brothers. I am quite sure it cannot be otherwise."

The sound of music from without, gave them to understand that the king was approaching. Presently the illustrious monarch of Chaldea made his grand entry, accompanied by a brilliant escort, and amid the flourishing of trumpets and the loud acclamations of his subjects he took his seat, and beckoned to the enthusiastic throng to be seated. Perfect stillness being secured, Ashpenaz arose with dignity, and, bowing low to the sovereign, proceeded:

"According to appointment, O king, behold these young men are conducted hither for public examination in the presence of their illustrious sovereign, and in the presence of these, his nobles."

To which the monarch replied in an interesting address:

"Citizens of Babylon! the king taketh much pleasure in greeting you on this occasion. To witness your smiles is truly refreshing to my mind amid all the pressing duties of my extensive empire. I trust I shall always merit your smiles and good wishes. Long may the Chaldean empire continue to shine a superior orb in the firmament of nations.

"The stability of government must greatly depend on the wisdom and intelligence of the people; and ever since I have had the honor of presiding over the destinies of this vast empire, I have not for a day lost sight of this important truth. Whether since the beginning of my reign the cause of education has been advanced, I leave to the judgment of my worthy subjects. Three years ago, I thought it advisable to establish a school at the expense of the government, where a number of young men might be placed under the care of superior instructors, and so be prepared to serve with distinguished ability in the different spheres in which they might be called to move. Those youths are now before you; and if their mental culture will well compare with their fair countenances and manly forms, my most sanguine expectations are more than realized. I am happy to know, from vigilant observation, that the teachers, without any exceptions, have nobly proved themselves worthy of the unreserved confidence of their king; and let them now be assured that such unwearied faithfulness will not go unrewarded. The king has been well pleased also, from time to time, to hear of the great proficiency and rapid advancement of many of the scholars."

It cannot be expected, on an occasion like the present, that all scholars will exhibit precisely the same amount of ability and cultivation. While all may give satisfaction, some, I trust, will even excel. Those who shall at this time give the clearest proof of ripe scholarship, shall, according to agreement, be permitted to remain at the palace, and minister in the presence of the king, with the prospect of promotion as the fruit of faithfulness. I trust there are no unpleasant feelings to arise from the final result of this day's exercises. True, there may be some disappointment among both parents and scholars; but let not the king be grieved by witnessing any signs of displeasure on the countenance of young or old; for, hitherto, no partiality hath been permitted in any of our councils. Those whom the king promotes must therefore be promoted on the strength of their own worth and merit.

"My worthy and noble friend, Ashpenaz, will now commence the examination; after which, if I think it expedient, I may ask a few questions myself."

Ashpenaz then, according to direction, commenced the examination, the king, in the meanwhile, earnestly facing the students, and paying particular attention to every answer, and the source whence it proceeded. After an examination of one hour, the king gave to Ashpenaz a signal, by which he understood that he might dispense with any further questioning.

The king then, as he had previously intimated, became the examiner. Being somewhat astonished, as well as delighted, by the perfect ease with which the youths of Judah answered every question, he purposed, within himself, to make a further trial of their skill, by propounding questions to the school which were far more difficult to answer than those asked by Ashpenaz. The reader is already aware that the king was one of the ripest scholars within the empire, and, therefore, was fully prepared for the undertaking. The first problem was directed to Shagoth. Shagoth colored, and, in endeavoring to answer, stammered out something which the king could not understand. The same question was directed to Apgomer. Apgomer, with steady voice and correct emphasis, answered; and it was pronounced to be correct. The next question was directed to Scribbo. He, greatly alarmed at the result of the other question, became confused, and gave no answer. The same question was directed to Daniel, and was promptly answered, with marked ease and great clearness. The next was directed to a young student who sat in the vicinity of Shagoth, but it was not answered to the satisfaction of the king. The same was directed to Hananiah, and the answer was such as to astonish the examiner. Another perplexing question was directed to a young student, a resident of the city; but it was of too profound a nature for the young man to answer. The king having asked the same question of several without receiving an answer, at last directed it to Azariah. The young Hebrew hesitated - it was but for a moment - then, in a clear, silvery tone, he gave the answer, without the least degree of confusion. It was beyond the expectation of the king. He gazed on the youth for a moment in silence, and then pronounced the answer to be a correct one. Another question of the same nature, requiring, perhaps, some additional knowledge, was asked, the king remarking, at the same time, that his good opinion of their abilities did not depend upon their answering those questions, for they were of such a nature as would puzzle more experienced heads; but such was the readiness with which some of the scholars had answered all the questions hitherto asked, that he was anxious to know if it were in his power to ask a question which they could not answer; and in order to give all an equal opportunity, he would direct his questions to each one. So the king commenced on the left, and deliberately pointed to each scholar; but no answer was heard until he came to young Mishael. With promptness, and in a few words, he gave a perfect answer to a question which the King of Babylon considered beyond the capacity of any student present.

By this time it was evident to the king that the number of those who truly excelled was four; and that these four sat together. To these, therefore, he would direct his remaining questions. And now, in earnest, commenced a regular contest for the mastery. On one hand, behold the great sovereign of the Chaldean empire, noted for the depth of his learning. On the other, behold four young men, from the land of Israel, whom, three years before, he had brought as captives of war from the metropolis of Judah. All the king's powers of mind were called forth. From the occasion he gathered a degree of enthusiasm, and he was glad of an opportunity to show himself to such pleasing advantage before so many of his nobles and influential subjects. With the four Hebrews he was highly delighted. Their great knowledge astonished him; but still he thought that soon he would be able to bring them to a dead stand. Question after question was asked, and question after question was answered, to the utter astonishment of the large audience. The contest was long, and of a thrilling nature; and not until the king was convinced that he was dealing with his superiors did he cry out, in a loud voice:

"It is enough!"

Every eye rested on Ashpenaz, as he stood ready to announce the names of those whom the king wished to honor.

"Belteshazzar!"

Daniel, with calm dignity and genuine modesty, left his seat, walked to the place appointed, and bowed low in the presence of the king.

"Shadrach!"

Hananiah, with a slight blush, that rendered him but the more comely, left his seat, and stood by the side of his cousin, in the presence of the king.

"Meshach!"

Mishael, with a smile on his lip, and an unfaltering step, found his place by the side of his brother.

"Abednego!"

Azariah, with a degree of paleness spread over his youthful countenance, left his seat, and joined his comrades.

"Apgomer!"

Apgomer was startled. The contented youth looked for no such result. Delighted with the triumph of the Hebrews, and the punishment of his cousins' vanity, he considered himself well rewarded. But, remembering himself, he quickly left his seat, and, with a pleasant smile upon his countenance, he took his place by the side of Azariah.

The parchment was rolled up and delivered over to the king.

The king arose, and thus addressed the five:

"Young men! Your honor cometh not from the king. It is the result of your own industry and perseverance. By the favorable interposition of the gods, ye have arrived at a perfection in knowledge never exhibited before on any occasion in the presence of the king. Four of your number are from another country. The hills of Judah are yet fresh in your memories, and Jerusalem is far from being forgotten. I have been well pleased, from time to time, to learn of your amiable deportment and noble bearing. Justice requires me to say that a peculiar perfection has been visible in all your past perfor-mances; and now, Belteshazzar, Shadrach, Meshach, and Abednego, youths of Judah, ye are, through the power and word of the king, elevated to share in all the immunities and privileges of Chaldean citizens. Long, by your superior wisdom and knowledge, may ye continue to shed additional luster on my already shining empire.

"Apgomer! Thou hast well sustained thyself throughout the examination; and, although thou hast not reached that lofty perfection manifested in the uniform answers of these, thy young friends from Judah, yet thou hast convinced the king that thou standest far above the level of thy fellows - as such thou art rewarded.

"The king findeth no fault with any. Ye have given proof of a good degree of mental strength, and I trust that from this place ye shall go forth to add to the stability and perpetuity of my empire.

"In conclusion, I command that Belteshazzar, Shadrach, Meshach, Abednego, and Apgomer be decorated with their appropriate badges, and conducted, with due honor, to their apartments at the palace. The examination is closed."

The merry blasts of trumpets followed this announcement. The king and his attendants first left the apartment; then followed the five youths, next the other students. Then the concourse dispersed as their various fancies dictated. The grand result was known, and, with few exceptions, it gave universal satisfaction. The superior wisdom of the young Hebrews was so abundantly evident, that no room was left for caviling; and each one was compelled to unite in the righteous verdict of the king. The amiable and modest deportment of the young Hebrews so won the affections of the spectators that when they were adorned with their badges of honor, they were loudly cheered.

Before they all disperse let the reader have the pleasure of a glimpse at a group of countenances that give unmistakable signs of genuine delight.

"Charming!" cried Joram, in ecstasies. "The reward of fidelity and perseverance, Barzello!"

# CHAPTER XV.

THE stately mansion of Barzello was brilliantly illuminated. Streams of light poured forth from every window. Sweet melody floated on the wings of the gentle zephyrs. Chariot after chariot arrived, and halted before the massive portals. It was evident to the passer-by that it was not an event of common occurrence that called forth such unusual movements and peculiar displays.

From the first moment of Mathias and Perreeza's introduction to each other, there was a warm attachment formed, and from the subsequent revelations, this sentiment greatly increased.

On this night the maid of Judah was to become the happy bride of Mathias; and from the smiles that greet smiles on the happy countenances of those who hurry to and fro through the richly furnished apartments, it is evident that their union is hailed as a joyous event.

The marriage was not, in all its parts, so strictly after the customs of the Hebrews as if it had been solemnized in the land of Judah. The long residence of Joram in Babylon, together with the very high regard he cherished for his friend Barzello and his family, gave the features of the occasion an admixture of Hebrew and Chaldean customs.

Never did the "Rose of Sharon" bloom fairer. Three years have added ripeness to her beauty, and dignity to her charms. She is no longer the timid maid of seventeen, but a blooming damsel, having reached her twentieth year, with a finish stamped on all her words and actions; and no one who has had the pleasure of her acquaintance can envy such a choice spirit the heart and hand of one of the most brilliant young men in the great metropolis.

The "Lily of the Valley" has but one thing to diminish her full share of enjoyment - and that is by no means a trifling one. Her sweet Perreeza, her constant companion for the last three years, whom she loves as her own sister, is about to leave her father's house and take her abode with another. This, at times, makes her sad. The same cause produces the same effect on Perreeza. She, also, is about to impress the parting kiss on the fair cheek of one who has proved herself worthy of her ardent love - one who gave her such a warm welcome to her large heart, when a stranger in a foreign land - one who has continued to love her with a pure affection. But these gloomy feelings are not to predominate at this time; so the "Lily" ceased to droop, and the "Rose" bloomed fresh and gay.

The announcement that Mathias, with his attendants, had arrived at the entrance, caused an exclamation of joy. Jupheena and a merry group of her maiden acquaintances formed themselves in procession, to meet them, and to escort the company, with warm congratulations, to the parlors, where they were received by Barzello with enthusiastic welcome, and conducted with appropriate honors to their apartments.

The ceremony was performed in a spacious room,

extending throughout the length of the grand edifice. The services were conducted by a Hebrew priest, who was brought to Babylon with other captives at the close of Jeconiah's reign of three months.

In entering the wedding apartment, one part of the company appeared at one end, while the rest at the same time appeared at the other end. Thus Mathias, with a band of young men, and Perreeza, with a group of damsels, slowly marched, met, and formed into a circle in the center of the room, the officiating priest, with a small altar, in the midst.

"Ye who are to take upon you the holy and solemn vows of matrimony, draw nigh," said the priest.

Without delay, the loving twain left the circle, and stood side by side before the sacred altar, when the priest, after a brief marriage ceremony, gave them this blessing: "God of Abraham, Isaac, and Jacob, keep, bless, and preserve you, and so fill you with all benediction and grace, that ye may walk before Him in the beauty of true perfection and holiness. Perreeza, daughter of Amonober, of the royal line of Judah, behold thy husband! Mathias, son of the illustrious Joram, behold thy wife! Take her as thine own, and convey her to thine own habitation, and there make merry with thy numerous friends."

At the house of Joram, preparations on a magnificent scale were made for the return of the bridegroom with his bride. A large number of the flower of the young men and maidens of Babylon were assembled, to congratulate the young pair on their happy union.

The bridegroom and bride led the train. They were

seated in a superb chariot, drawn by two spirited, snow-white steeds. The next was that of Barzello, containing himself and daughter, while a merry company brought up the rear. Nothing could have exceeded the beauty and brilliancy of the occasion. A flashing light from a hundred flaming torches completely banished the gloom of night, while hundreds of delighted spectators made the welkin ring with cheers. They soon reached the wide portals of Joram's mansion. The charioteers alighted. The bridegroom and bride first entered, the guests following in regular order. "They that were ready entered with him into the marriage, and the door was shut."

．　．　．　．　．　．．

The celebration was over. The company had retired. Quietude was restored. The Joram family, with one additional gem, was once more left to the peacefulness of its own mansion. They were all quietly seated. Joram arose, and slowly approached the old harp, the friend of his early days, and inspected it with fondness, while the thoughts of other years fast crowded upon his memory.

"My dear father, and my dear Uncle Esrom!" said Perreeza, smiling, "now that they are all gone, let us have one dear little song from thee."

"Ah, precious child!" said Esrom, at the same time brushing away a fugitive tear, "I play so seldom nowadays, I fear I would not appear to very good advantage among such fine performers."

" Nay, father! but thy playing is far superior to our best performances."

"Well, Perreeza, I will try; but I fear my song will make thee sad."

"Sadness at times, dear father, is far more profitable to the mind than hilarity."

"True, my daughter! True! We both know it by experience."

The Hebrew took the harp, and, in tones peculiar for their sweetness, sang a plaintive melody.

# CHAPTER XVI.

GREAT success attended the reign of the King of Babylon. His powerful legions had proved victorious in every clime. In addition to Judea, he had subjugated Egypt, Syria, Phoenicia, and Arabia. Peace once more was proclaimed, and the great body of the army was called home. The monarch's popularity was unbounded, and his praises were loudly trumpeted on the wings of every breeze, from east to west, and from north to south. The Chaldean empire rose still higher in glory, while numerous tributaries continued to pour their streams of gold into its already rich treasuries.

The afternoon was warm and sultry. The king reclined on an easy couch within a bower, in the palace garden. His mind was occupied with reflections on the past and thoughts of the future, and thus ran the soliloquy of the mighty potentate:

"Yea, the years are passing! On looking back they seem but short. But where has more been accomplished in so short a period? Ah, King of Babylon, thy career, hitherto, has been a brilliant one. My armies have clothed themselves with glory, which glory reflects back on their king. Surrounding nations do me homage. My coffers are filled from the wealth of Judah, Egypt, Syria, Phoenicia, and Arabia. What hinders my success? Babylon is but in the infancy of her greatness. Her glory shall yet reach the heavens! Tea, I will make her a fit place for the residence of the gods. Selfish? Yea, truly. And who ever succeeded without being selfish? Yea, the King of Babylon is selfish; but may the gods assist me to hide it from the people. To them, may it appear that all my efforts are put forth in their behalf. But have I no regard for the welfare of my people aside from my own glory? I have! The gods know I have. And yet, I have a strong desire that my name shall be carried down to posterity surrounded by a halo of glory. Is this selfishness? Be it so. It must be done! Am I not deep in the affections of my people? In this I cannot be mistaken. Never was the Chaldean empire so firmly established. It will stand forever. Forever? Ah, that word has a long meaning. But what power can overthrow us? Is not Babylon the mistress of the world? Is not Chaldea the queen of nations? Will not her prosperity be perpetual? Alas for our brief knowledge! The gods, in this, have not elevated the king above the beggar. The future is enshrouded in gloom and hid from the gaze of mortals. My wise men say that they can penetrate this gloom. Can they? I have my doubts. The future - the far, far future of Chaldea - I should be glad to know: but who shall sit on the throne one hundred years from to-day, and what shall be the greatness of Babylon in two hundred years, are questions which time alone must solve. Surely, this is a sultry day! Well, the future we cannot know. It may be all in wisdom. Peradven - Ah, sleep! thou art the great conqueror of conquerors. I surrender. Thy powers are irresistible. Let me not long be thy captive. In one hour, I pray thee, strike my chains asunder, and restore me to my friends."

And the king, quietly yielding to the stern demands of

Nature, was soon in the fast embrace of slumber.

. . . . . ..

"Oh, ye gods that dwell in light, what a dream!" cried the king, hastily leaving his couch, in agitation. "Oh, what a dream! But, alas, it has gone from me! Oh, ye gods, why have I not retained it? But can I not recall it to mind? Alas, it has fled! It has vanished! How perplexing! It was not a common dream. Nay, it bore particularly upon the future of my vast empire. And yet not one clear circumstance is retained in my memory. What shall I do? How shall the lost dream be restored? My astrologers profess to give the interpretation of dreams. If they can do this, why not as well restore the dream entire?"

And the king, in an agitated state of mind, left the garden and entered the palace.

"Arioch!" cried the king, "haste thee, and without delay let the most noted of the wise men and astrologers of Babylon be commanded to appear in my presence. Let there be no useless tarrying. My demands are urgent. Haste thee! Away!"

Without asking any questions, the astonished and half frightened officer hastened from the presence of his king, and gave all diligence in the performance of his urgent duty. He found ready access to the prince of the magicians, delivered to him the message of the king, and retired. The astrologer soon sent the message to his numerous companions, and in a short time the concentrated wisdom of the great metropolis stood in the presence of the king.

"Ye have done well," said the king, eying them with a degree of severity, "to be thus punctual; a failure on this point might have involved you in serious difficulties. Ye stand before the king as the representatives of wisdom. Ye profess to be able to bring to light hidden mysteries, and to make known the transactions of the future. The correctness of your professions is about to be tested. If it stands the ordeal, well; if not, woe be unto you!"

"All this thy servants profess," replied the chief astrologer, "and all this they can perform. Let them but learn the desire of the king, and they stand ready to execute his pleasure."

"This day," replied the king, "while slumbering on my bed, I dreamed a peculiar dream, and my spirit is troubled to know the vision."

"Oh, king, live forever!" replied the magicians, well pleased with the nature of their task. "Tell thy servants the dream, and we will show thee the interpretation thereof."

"Will ye, indeed!" answered the king, ironically. "But the thing has gone from me. I have no distinct remembrance of the various features of the dream. And now, as a proof that ye are able to give a correct interpretation, I demand that ye restore to my mind the dream in all its parts. Remember that ye are not able to impose on me a false vision. Now, proceed with your divination, and if in this ye fail, by the gods, ye shall be cut to pieces, and your houses shall be made a dunghill."

"Tell thy servants the dream, and we will show the

interpretation thereof," answered again the now astonished magicians.

"Ah, indeed!" said the king, disdainfully. "And have I not already told you that the thing is gone from me; and how can I tell you the dream? If I were able to do this, ye would readily produce your lying and corrupt interpretations. Do ye not profess to derive your knowledge and power of interpretation from the gods? Then let the same gods reveal unto you the dream itself."

"This is a strange demand, indeed," answered the alarmed astrologers. "There is not a man on earth that can grant thy desire, and show thee this matter. Be assured, O king, that thou requirest impossibilities at the hands of thy servants; and there is none other that can show it before the king, except the gods, whose dwelling is not in the flesh."

"And do ye not profess to hold intercourse with those gods?" answered the king, in a passion; "thus ye have proved yourselves to be a band of lying hypocrites. Begone from my presence, ye corrupt deceivers, and learn that your guilty career is near its close!"

So the terrified magicians were hurried from the presence of the passionate king, and by his orders were confined; and, moreover, a decree was issued, that all the wise men of Babylon should be put to death. Such was the unholy impulse of a king who had hitherto manifested, on most occasions, a commendable degree of self-possession.

The next day, while Daniel was walking in the vicinity of the palace, he was suddenly accosted by the captain of the guard, who informed him that it was his painful duty to apprehend him as an individual who was condemned to die by a late edict of the king.

"My worthy friend must certainly be mistaken in regard to the person," answered Daniel, with a smile; "for I am happy to know that in nothing have I transgressed the law of my sovereign."

"It would give me much pleasure on this occasion to find myself mistaken," replied Arioch, "but I fear that it will prove otherwise. Art thou not Belteshazzar, of the captivity of Judah, and art thou not numbered among the wise men?"

"And what can be the nature of my offense?" asked the young Hebrew, nothing daunted. "If in anything I have offended, I ask not to be spared."

"And hast thou not heard the decree?"

"No new decree has reached my ears."

"Then I shall communicate to Belteshazzar all I know concerning the matter." Which he proceeded to do.

"Many thanks to thee, kind officer. I have no desire to escape thy vigilance. Only permit me to see the king, and, peradventure, things may take a different course."

"Any favor I can show, without violating positive orders, will readily be granted. So I will make thy pleasure known to the king."

Arioch hastened into the presence of the sovereign, and informed him that one of the wise men prayed to be admitted into his presence.

"I desire not to see any of the vile race!" answered the king, with a frown. "I was satisfied yesterday that they are a band of lying impostors."

"May the king pardon his unworthy servant," replied Arioch; "but the young man that seeks thy face to-day was not among the number yesterday."

"And by what name is he known?" frowningly inquired the king.

"His name, O king, is Belteshazzar, of the captivity of Judah."

"Belteshazzar! Belteshazzar!" exclaimed the king, suddenly rising to his feet. "May the gods forgive me! Belteshazzar, whose wonderful display of wisdom astonished the city on the day of examination? Why did I not think of him sooner? Yea, and his three companions! and all at the palace! close at hand! and far superior in wisdom to all others! Belteshazzar! Yea, Arioch! By all means let the young Hebrew be admitted."

The captain of the guard hastened from the presence of the king to inform Daniel of his success.

"Belteshazzar, the king grants thy petition, and thou art requested to appear before him."

Daniel, with his usual calmness and dignity, walked into the presence of the king, while Arioch was beckoned to retire.

"Belteshazzar," said the king, "thou art thus admitted into my presence, and thou art at perfect liberty to speak freely on whatever subject mostly occupies thy mind. I have heretofore been well pleased with thy superior knowledge and wisdom, as well as that of thy comrades. The army has of late occupied the most of my attention, and among the various affairs of importance it is nothing astonishing if some of my best subjects are partially overlooked. Proceed with thy request."

"A little over four years ago, O king, according to thy direction, thy servant, with his three companions, was brought from the land of Judah to the great city of Babylon. Hitherto, we have been the subjects of thy kind regards. At thy expense we have been taught in all the learning and wisdom of the Chaldeans; and, in the presence of hundreds of thy worthy nobles, thou sawest fit to pronounce us superior in the various branches of learning, and, amid enthusiastic cheers, we were escorted to the palace of the king. We have endeavored to prove ourselves worthy of the favors and regard. We have spared no pains to render ourselves agreeable in the eyes of our superiors; and never have we heard a word of complaint. We have made no pretensions to superior wisdom. We are numbered among the wise by the direction of the king. In all things have we aimed to be thy faithful, loyal subjects. Judge then, O king, the astonishment of thy servant when, not half an hour ago, he was apprehended by the captain of the guard as one already appointed to death, according to the direction of the king. I wonder not that thine anger is kindled against the false pretensions of the magicians. But why should the innocent suffer with the guilty? And why, especially, should thy Hebrew servants die without, at least, a trial of their ability through the direct agency of their God, to restore to the king his lost dream? I, therefore, pray thee, O king, to give thy servant time, and the God that I worship will give me the knowledge of the dream and its interpretation."

"Belteshazzar," cried the king, "thy request is granted. Go! and may thy God give thee the knowledge of the vision."

Daniel left the presence of the king and hastened to join his comrades at their apartments.

"What now, fair cousin?" said Azariah. "What am I to learn from such a countenance? Nothing of a joyful nature, I fear!"

"Alas, comrades!" answered Daniel, "unless Jehovah interfere with a miraculous hand, we are undone. The decree has already gone forth from royal lips that all the wise men of Babylon must perish by the sword."

He then gave his companions a full history of the thing, as he had received it from the mouth of Arioch, the captain of the guard.

"In all our trials hitherto," said Hananiah, "we have found Jehovah to be our sure refuge. In him we trust, and he will surely open to us a way of escape."

"Already I feel the strange assurance that from this conflict we shall come forth triumphant," said Daniel.

"Most humbly will we all bow before our God, and pray that a clear revelation of the lost dream may be made on the mind of our beloved Daniel," said Azariah.

In solemn silence, the youths of Judah departed, and retired to their respective apartments, there to prostrate themselves before the Lord in humble devotion, with full confidence that the God in whom they trusted would hear their prayer and grant their petition.

Many hours had already passed away. Stillness prevailed throughout the thoroughfares of the great metropolis. Silence reigned throughout Babylon. The faithful night guardians solemnly paraded the streets in the performance of their important duties. The queen of cities was hushed to repose; its vast thousands had, for a while, forgotten their toil and sorrow. Old midnight was left far in the rear, and some faint signs in the eastern skies betokened the distant approach of day. But yonder, on their bended knees, see the trembling forms of Amonober's children! For many hours they have wrestled with God. Does He hear them? But where is Daniel? Let us silently enter his chamber. The son of Baramon is asleep! Mark his countenance!

Still the three brothers, "with their faces toward Jerusalem," are bowed before the Lord. But hark! Ah! it is the well-known voice of Daniel. It rings melodiously throughout every apartment and it falls on the ears of the cousins. Hark!

"Blessed be the name of God forever and ever, for wisdom and might are his. And he changeth the times and seasons. He removeth and setteth up kings. He giveth wisdom unto the wise, and knowledge to them that seek understanding. He revealeth deep and secret things. He knoweth what is in the darkness, and the light dwelleth with him. I thank Thee and praise Thee, O God of my fathers, who hast given me wisdom and might, and hast made known unto me now what we desired of Thee; for Thou hast made known to us now the king's matter."

Early in the morning, Daniel sought an interview with Arioch, and besought the reversing of the sentence against the wise men, and assured him that he was fully prepared to appear before the king, and restore to him the lost vision.

"Let Belteshazzar be assured," said the captain of the guard, "that I shall not move a finger against the wise men but by the positive orders of the king, and I am happy to say that he hath ordered me to delay execution until I receive further directions. I have just learned by chance that the merchant Joram has had an interview with the king in behalf of thee and thy friends. If I can be of any service to Belteshazzar, I am at his pleasure."

"In one hour, then, I will call on thee again, and thou shalt accompany me into the presence of the king," and Daniel departed.

Daniel found his companions sunk into calm slumber, from which they were not then awakened. He partook of a slight repast, bowed once more in adoration before God, and returned to seek Arioch, the captain of the guard.

They were soon on their way to the palace. Arioch first entered.

"O king, live forever! Belteshazzar is without, desiring

to see thee; and - "

"No more from thee at this time," interrupted the king. "Retire, and send the young man hither."

The officer, well used to the manner of his sovereign, bowed low and retired.

"Belteshazzar," said Arioch, "thou are admitted; and may the gods give thee success."

With a firm step, and a calm look, and with full confidence in the God of Israel, the Hebrew youth once more marched into the presence of the King of Chaldea.

"Belteshazzar," cried the king, "art thou able to make known unto me the dream which I have seen, and the interpretation thereof?"

"The secret which the king demandeth of his servant is far above the knowledge and comprehension of all his wise men, astrologers, magicians, and soothsayers. But the God of heaven - that Jehovah who dwelleth in light - he revealeth secrets, and maketh known to the king, Nebuchadnezzar, what shall come to pass in the latter days. Be it known, therefore, to the king, that this secret is not revealed to me through any wisdom that I have more than any living, but it is the kind interposition of Jehovah in behalf of thy servant and his companions in tribulation, who are doomed to die; and, moreover, to show the king that Jehovah is the only God.

"Thy dream, and the vision of thy head, are these: As for thee, O king, thy thoughts came into thy mind upon thy bed, what should come to pass hereafter; and He that revealeth secrets maketh known to thee the grand events of the future.

"Thou, O king, sawest a great image. This great image, whose brightness was excellent, stood before thee, and the form thereof was terrible. This image's head was of fine gold, his breast and arms of silver, his belly and thighs of brass, his legs of iron, his feet part of iron and part of clay. Thou sawest that a stone smote the image upon the feet which were of iron and clay, and brake them to pieces. Then was the iron, the clay, the brass, the silver, and the gold, broken to pieces together, and became like the chaff of the summer threshingfloor, and the wind carried them away, that no place was found for them; and the stone that smote the image became a great mountain, and filled the whole earth. This is the dream. Now, O king, listen to the interpretation thereof.

"Thou, O king, art a king of kings: for the God of heaven hath given thee a kingdom, power, strength, and glory; and wheresoever the children of men dwell, the beasts of the field, and the fowls of the heaven, hath he given unto thine hand, and hath made thee ruler over them all. Thou art this head of gold. And after thee shall arise another kingdom inferior to thee; and another third kingdom of brass, which shall bear rule over the earth. And the fourth kingdom shall be strong as iron, forasmuch as iron breaketh in pieces and subdueth all things; and as iron that breaketh all these, shall it break in pieces and bruise. And whereas thou sawest the feet and toes, part of potter's clay and part of iron, the kingdom shall be divided, but there shall be in it of the strength of the iron; forasmuch as thou sawest the iron mixed with clay, so the kingdom shall be partly strong and partly broken. And whereas thou sawest iron mixed with miry clay, they shall mingle themselves with the seed of men; but they shall not cleave one to another, even as iron is not mixed with clay. And in the days of these kings shall the God of heaven set up a kingdom which shall never be destroyed; and this kingdom shall not be left to other people, but it shall break in pieces and consume all these kingdoms, and it shall stand forever. Forasmuch as thou sawest that the stone was cut out of the mountain without hands, and that it brake in pieces the iron, the brass, the clay, the silver, and the gold, the great God hath made known to the king what shall come to pass hereafter: and the dream is certain, and the interpretation thereof sure."

For a while the king, in silent astonishment, gazed on the wonderful being before him; then he arose and fell prostrate at the feet of the captive Hebrew, and paid him adoration suitable only to a divine being.

"Let thy adoration be paid to Jehovah, O king!" cried Daniel, "for it is he that revealeth secrets, and bringeth to light the hidden mysteries."

"Of a truth, your God is a God of gods," cried the king, "and a revealer of secrets, seeing thou couldest reveal this mystery. And now, Belteshazzar, thou art exalted to be a ruler over the whole province of Babylon, and chief of the governors over all the wise men of Chaldea; and if thou desirest any particular favor, let it not be hidden from the king; for thou art worthy of all honors, and the full desire of thy heart shall be given thee."

"For himself, thy servant has nothing to ask; but be it

known to thee, O king, that thou art as much indebted for the restoration of the vision to my three companions as to thy servant, for in answer to our united prayers the secret was made known. I pray thee, therefore, that while I am thus honored, my companions may share in it."

"Wisely remarked. Thy three companions shall be promoted to posts of honor and trust in the empire. Let them, under thee, preside over the province of Babylon."

Thus Daniel, Hananiah, Mishael, and Azariah, through the miraculous interposition of that Jehovah they loved, and whose law they honored, were elevated to be the chief personages in the Chaldean empire.

# CHAPTER XVII.

YEARS passed by, and uninterrupted success attended the reign of the king of Babylon. The aggrandizement of the city was without a parallel in history. It appeared to have become the leading passion of the monarch's mind. The reader may have a faint idea of the glory of the city when he remembers that it was a regular square, forty-five miles in compass, enclosed by a wall two hundred feet high, and fifty broad, in which there were one hundred gates of brass. Its principal ornaments were the Temple of Belus, and the famous "hanging gardens."

The Temple of Belus was most remarkable for a prodigious tower that stood in the midst of it. According to Herodotus, it was a square, of a furlong on each side - that is, half a mile in the whole compass; and according to Strabo, it was a furlong in height. It consisted of eight towers, built one above the other; and because it decreased gradually towards the top, Strabo calls the whole a pyramid. It is not only asserted, but proved, that this tower far exceeded the greatest of the pyramids of Egypt in height.

The ascent to the top was by stairs round the outside. Over the whole, on the top of the tower, was an observatory, by means of which the Babylonians became more expert in astronomy than any other nation, and made, in a short time, the great progress in it ascribed to them in history.

In addition to these magnificent works, the public buildings of Babylon were counted by thousands, and its splendid mansions by tens of thousands.

The four Hebrews still continued in power, and more than retained their former excellence. Daniel was highly esteemed by the king for his great wisdom and skill in the affairs of government; but the impressions of the superiority of Jehovah, made upon the monarch's mind at the interpretation of the dream, had well-nigh been obliterated. Pride rebelled against the thought of the future overthrow of the empire; and fain would he have persuaded himself that uneasiness brought about by a troublesome dream was unworthy of him.

The three brothers, in their spheres, performed their duties with a degree of perfection and exactitude that greatly pleased the king; and for this, more than on account of their genuine excellence, were they regarded by him in a favorable light. Those pleasing qualities so apparent in the earlier history of the king were fast disappearing, to give way to pride, vanity, peevishness, and even cruelty.

The bold and impetuous declaration of the king, in regard to the sovereignty of the God of Israel, and the peculiar circumstances under which the poor Hebrews were promoted, were far from being forgotten by the Babylonians. There was a deep and abiding dissatisfaction in the minds of thousands in the realm, not so much on account of the elevation of the Hebrews, as on account of the conviction that the sovereign was not a sincere worshiper of the gods of the empire. The king, by occasional remarks from his nobles, had noticed more than once that there was something in their language that indicated a lack of confidence in his fidelity to the gods. Nebuchadnezzar, notwithstanding his increasing vanity, was far from being indifferent to the estimation in which he was held by his subjects. He knew that his safety was based on the confidence and friendship of his people, and he was determined, if by his former professions he had unwisely magnified the God of Daniel, and thereby lost the confidence of his Chaldean subjects, to give them unmistakable proof that he still was a worshiper at the shrine of Belus.

Summoning Belrazi, one of his most trusted officers, to his side, the king said:

"From the nature of thy position, thou art called to mingle in very numerous circles, and no man at the palace is better qualified than thou to judge of the feelings of the subjects toward their king. Come, now, be frank and plain with thy sovereign, and tell me how I stand in the estimation of my nobles."

"O king, live for ever!" replied the officer, highly delighted with this unusual mark of the king's confidence. "Thou livest in the warm affections of thy nobles, and in the pure regard of all thy numerous subjects. Thou art the peculiarly favored of the gods. All the nations of the earth fear thee, and pay their homage at thy feet."

"True. But art thou not aware that on one point my subjects are not as fully satisfied with their king as they might be? Behold, I have placed unusual confidence in my servant, and in return the king requireth equal sincerity."

"As thy soul liveth, O king, I shall hide nothing from thee. In mingling with thy nobles, I find that, without distinction, they are abundantly loyal. In a very few instances I have heard language that indicated that my lord the king was favorably inclined toward the God of the Hebrews, and less ardent in his devotion to the gods of Chaldea. But in this, has not my lord the king the perfect right to do as seemeth good in his sight?"

"The King of Babylon can do as seemeth good in his sight; and it shall seem good in his sight, not many days hence, to give abundant proof that the gods of Chaldea are the gods of the king. I am well satisfied with thy words. Let this interview, and others of the same nature which we may have, remain a secret. Thou mayest now leave, and to-morrow at the third hour be punctual to meet me again at this apartment."

The dignitary retired, and the king was left alone in his apartment.

"My suspicions were well founded! And, indeed, have they had no cause? Well, I was then young, and without experience. But was not the recovery of that dream a wonderful thing? Will anyone dare deny that? Had the God of Belteshazzar nothing to do with it? Again my thoughts are on the God of Israel! 'Tis hard to banish it from my mind! The interpretation was natural, and perfectly consistent. But I swear by the gods, that it shall not come to pass! I will establish my empire on such a sure foundation that it shall not be in the power of mortals to shake it. Are not the nations at my command? Are not my armies stationed on every shore? Is not Babylon the terror of kings? Ah! where is the power that can compete with Chaldea? My nobles are jealous of my fidelity to the gods. Yea, truly, and have I not given them reason?

"This must go no further. If I have some lingering fears of the God of Belteshazzar, it must not be made manifest. In this I must regain the full confidence of the nation. Are they jealous of the four Hebrews? In this I fear them not. They are worth more to my empire than any chosen score of their fellow-officers. And of the wisdom of my wise men - is not more than one half of it centered in Belteshazzar? If they are envious of these young men, let it not be known to the king, or by the powers of Belus I will let them feel my vengeance!

"But for the king to be suspected of being a believer in their God is of a more serious nature. What measure shall I resort to in order to satisfy the mind of the nation? Deny the insinuation in a proclamation? Shall the King of Babylon ever stoop to this? Never! Something more consistent with royal dignity than this must be found. An image? Yea! That will do, O king! Thou hast well thought. An image of Bel. What? 'With the head of gold, the breast and arms of silver, the belly and thighs of brass, the legs of iron, the feet of iron and clay?' Nay! The image of Bel which I shall set up for public worship, shall be all of gold. Why otherwise? My wealth is inexhaustible. Who, after such a display, would ever suspect the King of Babylon of adhering to the God of the Hebrews? This, then, is my purpose. I shall build a great image of Bel, made of pure gold, and set it up in some favorable spot, and appoint a day for its public dedication."

The next morning, at the appointed hour, Belrazi was punctual to meet the king at his apartment. The monarch, well pleased with his scheme of the image, manifested a pleasant countenance.

"Thou art punctual, Belrazi. The king is well pleased to meet thee. Thy frank sincerity yesterday was an additional proof of thy worth. I have seen fit, since we parted, to bestow some thought on the subject on which we conversed. It is of the utmost importance to the well-being and security of the empire that the people have unbounded confidence in their king in all things - in matters of religion as well as in matters of state. Now, in order to expel all doubts from the minds of my nobles in regard to my fidelity to the gods of my fathers, I have thought of a measure which, I trust, must prove successful. It is this: Let an image of our god Bel be made of gold. Let it be of large dimensions, and far superior to any image heretofore seen in any country. Let it be set up in some favorable spot; and on the day of its dedication, let all who hold office under the government, be commanded, by a royal decree, to appear on the spot, and, at the appointed hour, fall down and worship it; and let the penalty of disobedience be death. Let those who dare set at naught the will of the king be taken and thrown into the burning fiery furnace. What thinkest Belrazi of this?"

"O king, live forever! Thy goodness is unbounded. Thy design is dictated by that wisdom that cometh from the gods. The measure shall be hailed throughout the empire with shouts of rejoicing, and the day of its dedication will be a day of days in the future history of Chaldea."

"Let no time be lost, then," replied the king. "Let my head goldsmith be called, and from the lips of the king let him receive instructions in regard to the making of the image. This is my desire. Let the measure be known but to a few, until the proclamation shall go forth."

The head goldsmith was soon in the presence of the king, and after much deliberation the exact dimensions of the great image were settled upon; and, moreover, it was agreed, that by a certain day it should be completed.

According to the direction of the king, no publicity was given to the measure. Few of the king's confidential friends were apprised of it. In the meantime, no pains were spared by the chief goldsmith to have everything in readiness by the time appointed. Hundreds of the craft were called together to speed the great undertaking; and, even before the time agreed upon, the idol was ready to be set up. Word was sent to the king, and immediately the proclamation was trumpeted far and wide, throughout the length and breadth of the vast empire:

"Nebuchadnezzar, King of Babylon, to all his Princes, Governors, Captains, Judges, Treasurers, Counselors, Sheriffs, and all rulers of his provinces: Ye are hereby commanded to appear on the twenty-third day of the eighth month, at the third hour of the day, in the plain of Dura, within the province of Babylon, to witness the dedication of the great image which I have set up in honor of Bel, the god of the Chaldeans. Ye are, moreover, hereby commanded, at the hour appointed, to fall down and worship the golden image. Disobedience will be punished with the utmost rigor. Those who shall refuse to bow and worship shall in that same hour be taken and thrown into a burning fiery furnace.

"Given under my hand and seal, at the great City of Babylon, on this the fourth day of the seventh month.

"Nebuchadnezzar."

The dedication of the great image now became the chief theme of conversation. In city and village, on hill and in dell, in the palace and cottage, it was the leading subject; and throughout the empire it gave universal satisfaction. The measure for the time being had its desired effect - to establish in the minds of the Chaldeans the conviction that the king was faithful to the gods.

This proclamation was received by the three Hebrews with profound astonishment and deep regret. For many years now they had enjoyed tranquility and Worshiped the God of their fathers in calm simplicity; and this was the first time, since they came to Babylon, that they were required to do violence to their conscience by worshiping a false god. Daniel, on business of great importance, was sent to Egypt.

The three worthies soon met for the special purpose of deciding upon a course of action to be followed in the approaching emergency. No fearful apprehensions could be read in those countenances. No fainting fear took hold of their spirits. Their eyes sparkled with holy courage, their cheeks flushed with noble emotions, their forms were unusually erect. They were fully prepared for the worst.

The opening remarks were from Hananiah.

"Well, brothers, another cloud seems to darken our skies, and to hang threateningly over our heads; but I trust that, as servants of the Host High, we have by this time learned to gaze upon such things without terror or alarm. We are now assembled together to take a calm, sober look at the thing as it really is, and decide on our future course. We are surely much indebted to the king. For a number of years, we have been the recipients of his bounty and the objects of his kind regard, for which, undoubtedly, we all feel grateful. But the question is this: is it our duty, as the professed worshipers of the God of Israel, to yield obedience to the demand of an unholy and wicked law, that throws insult into the face of the God of heaven, and the Jehovah of the universe? In this case, either obedience or disobedience must be pleasing to God. Is it the will of Jehovah that we should obey this law, or disobey it? To my mind, it is clear that, in this case, nothing short of a manly disobedience can be agreeable to the will of our God. Brothers, we must have decision of character. In this matter there must be no compromise with iniquity."

And Hananiah took his seat with a smile of holy satisfaction playing on his lips, when Mishael arose, and said:

"The question rests here, brothers! Can any edict from any king, potentate, or human power, make null and void the laws of the eternal God? To this question, from us, there is but one short answer, and that is, 'Nay!' Is He not higher than the highest? Are not His commands far superior to all human edicts? The law of Jehovah is supreme, and let the higher law be obeyed, though the heavens should fall! Azariah, what sayest thou?"

"I say I shall not bow to any god but the God of Israel! In Him I trust. If we perish by the hand of our enemies, so let it be! Better death than a base betrayal of our sacred trust. But is not that God who saved us once from death able to deliver us again? Is his arm shortened, that he cannot save? Then let them heat the fiery furnace! That God in whom we trust will yet deliver us from this calamity, and overrule this dark providence to his glory."

A knock was heard. The door was opened, and the pleasant voice of the newcomer gave them to understand that he was no other than the kind-hearted Apgomer.

"I trouble you, at this time, as a bearer of dispatches from my kind master, Belteshazzar, who is now in Egypt, on government business of pressing importance. Before he left, he gave me positive orders to deliver all messages to his cousins without the least delay."

"Thou art ever welcome, dear Apgomer!" answered Hananiah. "and especially to-day, as a bearer of a dispatch from one we love so well."

"And here is another, from one that, peradventure, ye love the more. Ye perceive that the children of Judah have some confidence in their Chaldean friend."

"And great is the confidence thou deservest, as one that has proved himself a genuine friend in every trial," said Azariah.

"Let not my noble friend speak thus!" said the modest Chaldean, "for I deserve it not. I must return, and any further dispatches that may be sent to my care shall, without delay, be conveyed hither. Adieu!"

These dispatches proved to be letters. The last delivered was confidentially handed to Apgomer by Mathias, and was written by Perreeza.

The letter from Daniel was first considered. It was read aloud by Azariah.

"Ever Dear Cousins: I have this moment read the wonderful proclamation of the king, in regard to the great image of Bel, to be dedicated on the plains of Dura. By some strange providence, he saw fit to send me hither, with imperative instructions to remain until some unpleasant affairs between the two governments are amicably adjusted; and before this can be accomplished, the great idolatrous display will have passed. Your minds, undoubtedly, have been much troubled in view of the unpleasant position in which ye are placed. So hath the mind of your beloved cousin. Already I know full well that, with holy courage, ye are ready for the trial. The flames of a fiery furnace must fail to frighten a true Israelite from the worship of the God of his fathers. Past favors are not to be repaid by proving traitors to the God of Israel. We are the temporal subjects of the King of Babylon it is true, and in anything that interferes not with the command of Jehovah, we are happy to render him willing obedience: but with us obedience to the higher law is paramount to all other considerations. The words of a loving mother are yet fresh in my mind. The morning on which we left our beloved Jerusalem, she called me to her apartment, and, among a multitude of other good things, she said, 'The same integrity to the law of thy God will certainly secure thy prosperity among strangers. Thy path may occasionally be obstructed; but trust in God, my son, and all will be well. The land whither thou goest is a land of universal idolatry, where the God of thy fathers is not known, and where his worship may cause universal ridicule. Heed them not. With thy face toward Jerusalem, let thy petitions daily ascend to the God of Abraham, and he will direct thy paths. Never prove a traitor to the religion of thy fathers. My son will be obedient to the laws of his king that do not come in contact with his religion; but if ever thou art required to render obedience to any law that clashes with the law of thy God, remember, my son, that disobedience to that law must be rendered, even unto death if required. Let "Obedience to the Higher Law" be thy motto; for thy mother would sooner hear of thy death as a martyr to the religion of Judah, than of thy promotion to a throne by apostasy.'

"These burning words of your Aunt Josepha, to her son Daniel, are the words of Daniel to his cousins. Prove true to your religion! and if in this ye die, it shall be but the will of your God. But, cousins, ye shall not die! That same Jehovah who appeared in our behalf years ago, in the revelation of the king's dream, will again stretch out his arm to save. If Jehovah interferes in your behalf, there is not fire enough in all Chaldea to injure a hair of your head. I long to be with you! Nothing would give me greater pleasure than to be immediately called back to Babylon. Then side by side would we stand erect, and scorn to bow before a golden image. But it appears to be the will of Jehovah that I should be absent. I have confidence that I shall soon embrace you in Babylon: but if in this I am mistaken, we soon shall meet in the better Jerusalem above.

"Daniel."

It was with some difficulty that Azariah commanded sufficient control over his feelings to enable him to read the letter aloud; but with a trembling accent it was done.

"Thanks be to Jehovah." cried Mishael, "for such consolation in the midst of sore affliction."

"But what says our beloved Perreeza?" said Hananiah.

No one felt willing to read aloud their sister's letter, so it was read by each in silence. It ran thus:

"Dear Brothers: With emotions indescribable, Perreeza endeavors to write these few lines, that may impart some consolation to her dear brothers while strong waves of affliction pass over their souls. Being much confined of late to my dwelling, it was but yesterday that I derived any knowledge of that awful proclamation of the king in regard to his great image. Uncle Esrom is at present traveling in a far country on important business, and I am deprived of his counsel and ye are deprived of his aid in this crisis. Ob, my brothers! the companions and guardians of my juvenile hours, into whose care and warm affections I was committed by the parting words of a dying mother! How ardently does your sister love you! how deep for you is the affection of Perreeza's heart! What can I say that will cause one sweet ingredient to drop into your bitter cup? Nothing better do I know, than the favorite sentence of our beloved Jeremiah. If the good prophet were here would he not say, 'Jehovah is the strength of all his saints; trust in him and be at peace!' Oh, how sweetly flowed the gentle words of the man of God!

Brothers! dear as ye seem to my throbbing heart, terrible as the fiery furnace may rage, Perreeza has no desire that your safety should be purchased at a dishonorable price. Nay, brothers! if for a moment I should indulge in such an unholy desire, that moment I should forfeit all right to call you brothers. I shall not even advise you to stand firm in the fiery trial. Ah! too well do I know that your noble souls already scorn the command of an apostate king, who once acknowledged the supremacy of the God of Israel.

"My precious Jupheena came to see me this morning, and she is very confident that the God in whom we trust will bring you through this trial triumphantly. Dear brothers, accept this hasty dispatch as an offering of pure affection. Farewell, until our next meeting."

"Perreeza."

With full hearts, the brothers bowed before the Lord and rolled their burdens upon the Almighty. The entire consecration was now made, and they were ready for the trial. The struggle was over and their minds became as calm and tranquil as a summer evening.

# CHAPTER XVIII.

IN AN extravagantly furnished apartment of a fine-looking mansion in the heart of the city, sits a family group, consisting of a father, mother, two sons, and one daughter. They are far from exhibiting in their countenances that contentment of mind which is a "continual feast," and yet something has transpired that gives them, for the time being, an unusual degree of pleasurable emotion.

The father leaves his seat, and with folded arms he begins to pace slowly backward and forward the length of the apartment with an air of pompous dignity, while ever and anon a smile of extreme selfishness plays on his lips. He has received intelligence which he considers by no means displeasing.

The mother, to whom nature has been rather niggardly in the endowment of outward charms, is loaded with a superabundance of golden ornaments, in the vain attempt to supply the lack of the natural with the artificial. In her eye you look in vain for intelligence, or in her countenance for benevolence; but she smiles! yea, indeed, with something the mother is evidently pleased.

The two sons, in making a declaration of their brotherhood to a stranger, would stand in no danger of being suspected on that point as deceivers. The resemblance is quite striking.

The daughter is beautiful - in her own estimation. To this she clings as an essential part of her creed - that she constitutes a very important share of the beauty of Babylonia, but in getting it implanted into the creed of others, she proves unsuccessful - her converts being wholly confined to her father's household. She also, with the rest, on this night manifests an unusual degree of hilarity.

"Ah! they are ensnared at last!" said Scribbo, with an air of triumph. "They must either deny their religion or face the furnace. This is right, and happy am I that the king has at last seen fit to enact a law that will bear with stringency on those pretending foreigners who fill the most important stations in the government."

"But, brother," said the sister, eagerly, "which thinkest thou they will choose - the worship of our gods or the fiery furnace?"

"I am in hopes they are fanatical enough to choose the latter," answered the brother; "for in case they should choose the former, they would be as much in our way as ever. But then it would be some consolation to know that they had been compelled to worship and bow before the gods of the Chaldeans."

"There is one thing to be deeply regretted," said Shagoth. "I am informed that Belteshazzar, the great Rab Mag, is now in Egypt, and is not expected to return for some weeks. He also ought to bear them company and share the same fate. But if only we can put these three out of our way we shall have abundant reason to adore the gods."

"But, my sons," said the mother, "will not these Hebrews elude notice among so many? The gods know how I fear lest after all they may escape."

"Fear not that, mother," answered Scribbo. "Shagoth and myself will so arrange matters as to be near them; and if they bow not with us we will on the spot report them to the king."

"This is a matter of ponderous importance, and of immense consequence," said the promenading father. "From this, Chaldea shall hereafter reap abundant harvests. These proud and insolent foreigners who insinuate themselves into offices which native Chaldeans ought to fill, will now learn a lesson of modesty to which they have hitherto been strangers. Far better for our beloved Chaldea if the superstitious brood had been left in their own country. May the gods grant that every Hebrew office-holder may so cling to his imaginary god as to walk straight from office into sure destruction. My motto is 'Chaldeans for Chaldea!' Personally, I have no hostility toward these young men. Nay! But, O my country! my country! it is for thee my heart bleeds! Sons! ye shall do well to be on your guard, and see to it that they escape not your vigilance. If they die, their offices will be vacant, and must soon be supplied by some persons of ability. O my country! It is for thee, O Chaldea! my heart bleeds!"

"But," said the anxious mother, "are not these important offices at the disposal of the Rab Mag? If he still remains, can we expect any favors from him? Alas! my husband may well cry, 'O my country!'"

"Perhaps," said the daughter, "if he hears of the death of his companions, he will never return, but flee over the mountains to his own country."

"A trivial mistake, my daughter," said the patriot; "his country would lie in an opposite direction."

"But could he not change his course?" asked the half-offended daughter.

"Yea, verily, my child, if he should find that he was in the wrong path; peradventure, this would constitute his first business."

"I can hardly hope for such a happy result, sister," said Shagoth. "The conniving demagogue will cling to his office until compelled by a stringent law to abandon it."

"Before many days, the Rab Mag will return," said the erect promenader. "And will not the king ere long set apart another day for the public worship of the gods? And if this foreign pretender escapes now, justice will overtake him then. The vengeance of our deities will not always slumber, and these worshipers of other gods shall soon know that the best offices in our government and the best interests of our beloved country are not to be entrusted to a horde of superstitious foreigners. O my country! Sons! let me caution you again to be on the watch for these three rulers. They hold important offices, and such a favorable opportunity is not to be lightly regarded. O my country, my country!"

. . . . . . .

The day appointed for the dedication of the great

image at last arrived. Its ushering in was hailed by the populace with universal enthusiasm, marked by shouts of rejoicing. The day was fair and beautiful. No threatening cloud was visible in the heavens. The metropolis, at a very early stage, presented one grand scene of activity and preparation. The soldiery were out by thousands, their glittering panoply dazzling in the clear sunbeams. Officers of all grades hurried to and fro with excitement visible on their countenances. Those swarming thousands were evidently expecting some signal, at which they were ready to march. The word of command was at last given, and the multitude moved forward.

Onward the mighty concourse moved through the principal thoroughfares, amid the ringing of bells, the blasts of trumpets, and the waving of banners, until they arrived in a spacious square in front of the royal palace. Here they halted.

At last, the massive portals were thrown open, and the king, in a magnificent chariot, surrounded by an imposing guard, made his appearance. He waved his hand in the direction of the multitude, when, with one voice, the people exclaimed:

"O king, live forever!"

The procession was soon on its way to the plains of Dura, the king leading the pompous train, while eager thousands brought up the rear. On the way, they were joined by thousands more, who at different places waited their arrival, and at every stage the high praises of the King of Babylon echoed from ten thousand voices.

The great image far surpassed anything of its kind within the realm. Its dimensions were large and well proportioned, its height being twenty cubits, and its breadth six cubits, elevated on a richly gilded pedestal, forty cubits in height, thus being perfectly visible to all the worshipers. Around its base stood the officiating priests of Belus, with solemn visages, their long flowing robes adorned with numerous articles of rich regalia.

Scribbo and Shagoth, faithful to their revengeful promise, were on the keen alert for the three Hebrews. In their wanderings they came across Apgomer.

"We are in search of thy three Hebrew friends," said Shagoth. "Canst thou inform us where we may find them?"

"I can," promptly replied Apgomer. "I know the exact spot on which they stand."

"This is truly gratifying," replied Scribbo. "Now lead us to the spot without delay."

"To my Hebrew friends your presence would be anything but agreeable; and, as I am under far more obligations to them than to some others, I am very happy to disregard your request."

"Thou art in command of the same daring insolence as characterized thy school-days," said Scribbo, in an angry tone.

"To be accused of insolence by the envious sons of Skerbood, is fully equivalent to being called noble and gentle by a worthy citizen," answered Apgomer, with a smile of contempt playing on his lip. "So permit me to thank you for the high compliment."

"Speakest thou so to us, thou insulting pretender!" cried Shagoth, in a rage. "Thou hadst better depart ere we punish thy insolence with the edge of the sword."

"Terrible words, surely, from mighty swordsmen!" said Apgomer, smiling. "Is it any wonder I tremble beneath your gaze? Even from the days of your childhood your courage and valor have been proverbial. My cousin Scribbo, at the early age of ten years, would, without fear, push headlong into the water little girls years younger than himself; while the brave Shagoth, at the early age of twelve, could find no more pleasing recreation than to scourge his poor relatives of eight years old and under. Then ye were heroes in embryo; and now, having grown up, is it any wonder that the whole realm quakes beneath your tread? Hail! all hail, ye mighty sons of Skerbood! This is the day in which ye look for the full realization of your guilty hope, in the death of three of the choicest noblemen that ever adorned the Chaldean realm. Be not too sure of your prey. Strange things have appeared in those young men's histories, and more strange manifestations may yet appear."

"Too long already have we listened to thy insolent and silly harangue," said Scribbo. "Right glad are we that these foreign pets, who have so long been dandled on the lap of royalty, are at last brought to the test. We only hope that their fanaticism may lead them to disobedience. In that event, we would ask for no greater pleasure than to be permitted to throw them into yon blazing furnace."

"Ye are surely well adapted for such an undertaking. By all means, volunteer your services; and remember that, in the midst of your burning patriotism, these young foreigners hold responsible offices, that must be filled by some competent personages."

"Away, Scribbo, from the sound of this barking dog!" said Shagoth. And the two office-seekers hurried away in search of the doomed Hebrews.

They had gone but a little distance when they saw the three brothers together, a few rods on the left from the throne. The two Chaldeans, unobserved, stationed themselves close behind them, and there waited for the grand result.

Soon, a signal was given for the throng to come to silence and order. This was not easily accomplished. At length, however, order was fully gained, and breathless silence reigned over half a million of idolaters. This silence was broken by the loud accents of heralds, who passed through all parts of the assembly, crying at the top of their voices:

"To you it is commanded, O people of all nations and languages, that at what time ye hear the sound of the flute or harp, ye fall down and worship the golden image that Nebuchadnezzar the king hath set up. And whoso falleth not down and worshipeth shall the same hour be cast into a burning fiery furnace."

The heralds returned to their places, and their voices were no longer heard.

The grand signal was given! The musical instruments poured forth their loud strains, and the great mass fell prostrate before the glittering idol. But, yonder, behold those champions of moral integrity! Only three among five hundred thousand! While all besides have bowed the knee, there they stand! Their figures are heroic, their forms are erect, their arms folded, while an involuntary smile of contempt plays on their lips.

"By the gods, we have them!" whispered Shagoth, in ecstasies. "Behold, Scribbo, how erect their posture!"

"Hold thy peace!" whispered Scribbo, in return, "or they will hear us. When we rise, then we will confront them to good advantage. Thanks to the gods, they have well favored us."

The signal for the vast throng to arise from their worshiping attitude was given. No sooner was it heard, than Scribbo and Shagoth walked with an air of conscious triumph and stood before the three Hebrews.

"And who are these presumptuous and rash mortals," said Shagoth, "who thus dare to set the laws of the king at defiance? Tremble, ye daring wretches! for who are ye to withstand the vengeance of our sovereign?"

"To the king, then, we are accountable; and not to thee, thou crawling reptile," answered Hananiah. "So haste thee away; and if thou hast any authority, let it be displayed within its own sphere."

"Ah!" cried Shagoth, "ye are doomed to die! See ye not the heated smoke of the fiery furnace? Your guilty and rash conduct shall be made known to the king without delay. Your guilty career is well-nigh run; and Chaldea shall soon be delivered from the curse of foreign office-holders."

"But not from the curse of a groveling, envious, unprincipled horde of office-seekers," said Azariah, casting a withering glance on the two brothers.

"Away, brother!" cried Scribbo. "For why should we hear the abusive harangue of these overfed demagogues?"

And away the patriots hurried with their complaint to the king.

The monarch was surrounded by a large number of his nobles, who were loud in their congratulations at the complete success that had crowned the day.

An officer in uniform came forward, and bowed low in the presence of the king.

"What is thy pleasure, Arioch!" asked Nebuchadnezzar.

"Two men have approached the guard, O king, greatly desiring to be admitted into thy presence."

"Let them be admitted!" was the answer.

With anything but ease of manner, Scribbo and Shagoth walked into the royal presence.

"And what have ye to communicate?" inquired his majesty, eying them as if not quite satisfied with their appearance.

"O king, live forever!" replied the Chaldeans. "Thou, O king, hast made a decree that every man shall fall down and worship the golden image; and whoso falleth not down and worshipeth should be cast into a fiery furnace. There are certain Jews whom thou hast set over the affairs of the province of Babylon - Shadrach, Meshach, and Abednego - these men, O king, have not regarded thee; they serve not thy gods, nor worship the golden image which thou hast set up."

Then was the king full of wrath and fury. "What!" said he, "is my royal decree to be thus set at defiance? Is this the return they make to the king for their high promotion in the government? By all the gods, I will bend their stubborn wills, or they will suffer my vengeance to the uttermost! Let them be summoned into my presence without further delay!" And officers were soon on their march to bring the offenders.

The king, from his elevation, saw them approaching. An innocent smile rested on each countenance; and in spite of his haughty arrogance, the king's heart was touched, and his better feelings for a while triumphed. They stood in his presence, and respectfully, as usual, made their obeisance.

"Am I rightly informed, O Shadrach, Meshach, and Abednego," said the king, "when I hear that ye do not serve my gods, nor worship the golden image that I have set up? It may be true; yet for your sakes, I will give you one more trial: but beware that ye further provoke not my displeasure! The king's command is not to be trifled with!"

Without the least betrayal of fear, Hananiah, in a firm tone of voice, addressed the monarch:

"O king, it requireth no careful deliberation in this matter. In so plain a case the answer is ready at hand.

Thy servants, as thou well knowest, are natives of Judah, and we worship no god but the God of our fathers. As foreigners, we have at all times been careful to use no disrespectful language in regard to the gods of Chaldea, or those who pay them homage; and hitherto, unmolested, have we paid our simple adoration to the Lord God of Israel. The law of our God, with us, is regarded as infinitely superior to all human edicts. In all things pertaining to the government, we have faithfully endeavored to do thy will, and obey the directions of our sovereign. But not until this day have we been required to deny our religion, and insult our God. To thee, O king, we are much indebted. For many years have we been the objects of thy kind regard. But be it known to Nebuchadnezzar, that the continuance of his favor is not to be purchased by a base betrayal of our principles, or a denial of our God. We cannot serve thy gods, nor worship the golden image which thou hast set up. We bow the knee to God Most High alone! To us thy fiery furnace has no terrors! Jehovah, in whom we trust, is able to deliver us. That God who divided the Red Sea in two parts and made Israel to pass through the midst of it, and who parted the waves of the swelling Jordan, is able to preserve thy servants alive in the midst of the devouring flames! Yea, he will deliver us out of thy hand, O king! But, if in this we are mistaken, be it known unto thee, that toe can never obey any law of man that requireth a violation of the law of God. Therefore, we refuse to serve thy gods, or worship this golden image which thou hast set up."

"Seize the ungrateful wretches!" cried the king, in a rage, while paleness spread over his countenance. "Seize all who set my authority at naught, and who thus insult their king! By the gods, now shall they feel

Erasmus W. Jones

the weight of my displeasure, and reap the reward of their daring insolence! Let the furnace be heated seven times hotter than usual. Let the worthless dogs be thrown in, and let their God, if he be able, prove himself superior to the gods of Chaldea! Bind them now, in my presence!"

The three brothers were seized on the spot by several strong men, and bound hand and foot with cords. When this was done, they were conveyed in the direction of the fiery furnace. The news soon spread throughout the assemblage, and pressing thousands urged their way towards the place of execution. The fire raged with fury. Fagot after fagot was thrown in. The flames leaped high above the top of the black walls that surrounded them. The executioners were strong men of the royal guard. To these were added a number of others, who, to show the strength of their patriotism, volunteered their services. Foremost among these were Scribbo and Shagoth. With what triumphant malignity they gazed on the bound Hebrews! How complete they considered their own victory!

The word of command was given, and the victims were dragged up the massive steps that led to the upper edge of the burning pit. In this the volunteers showed more than an ordinary degree of patriotism. The Hebrews were laid side by side, ready for their awful doom. The stout hearts of the soldiers were touched with pity as they gazed on the noble forms of their victims, of whom they had never heard aught but good; and they felt loath to perform the awful deed. But not so the patriotic sons of Skerbood.

"Why not throw the guilty rebels in?" cried Shagoth, with an air of importance.

"As ye appear to take far more pleasure in this transaction than we do, we are very willing to bestow the honor of throwing them in on yourselves. So proceed with your delightful performance," said an officer, at the same time giving way, while his companions followed him some two or three steps downward.

"With all pleasure!" answered Scribbo, while, with fiendish eagerness, they both turned to perform the foul deed. With a firm grasp they first laid hold on Azariah, and he was thrown into the midst of the flames. The same was done to Mishael; and, finally, as Hananiah dropped to the burning depth below, the ascending flames became doubly fierce; at the same moment the wind shifted and became strong, and, as sudden as a flash of lightning, the flames poured their awful vengeance on the guilty heads of Scribbo and Shagoth. For a moment they whirled in the midst of God's avenging scourges, crying loudly for help; but no help could be administered! In another instant they became bewildered, and soon their blackened forms fell on the edge of the furnace, where a few moments before had lain the sons of Judah!

The king had not accompanied the prisoners to the fatal spot, but continued, in a surly mood, to sit on his elevated throne. He was far from being satisfied, and he inwardly regretted his severity toward the best of his officers.

The furnace was a roofless inclosure, twenty feet square, built of very thick walls in solid masonry. At the height of about twenty-five feet from the ground, on the inside, there were ponderous bars of iron, which were made to cross each other at right angles, and which fastened in the walls, forming the bottom of the furnace into which the victims were thrown from above. Below, in different parts, were appropriate places for fagots and light combustibles wherewith to heat the furnace. To the lower story there were eight doors or openings, two on each square, through which easy access was obtained to the fireplaces. On the outside there was but one entrance to the top. This was by means of massive stone steps. The depth from the edge of the furnace to the crossbars below was fifteen feet, making the whole height, from the ground, forty feet. From above also, there were steps to descend into the bottom. To spectators, on the ground, the victims were not visible after they had been thrown over the edge.

The king unwillingly turned his eyes towards the fiery furnace, and from his elevation he could see its interior. He suddenly sprang to his feet, lifted his hands on high, and exclaimed, in affrightened tone:

"O ye gods, what do I behold! What do I behold, O ye gods!" Then, turning to his nobles, he exclaimed: "Do I fancy, or is it real? Turn your eyes on yonder flames! In their midst what behold ye? Speak!"

The nobles tremblingly replied:

"We see men walking unhurt in the midst of the fire, O king!"

"It is even so!" cried the monarch, in deep agitation. "It is not a delusion! It is a marvelous reality! But did we not cast in three men bound? And I see four men loose walking in the midst of the fire, and they have no hurt! And the form of the fourth is like unto a son of the gods! Arise, let us hasten to the spot!"

The king, attended by a number of his nobles, and surrounded by the royal guard, was soon on his way towards the furnace. The thronging masses divided to give way to their sovereign. There were but few there that knew the cause of the king's agitation. Those who witnessed his countenance attributed it to the awful death of Scribbo and Shagoth.

All eyes are fastened on the king. With a hurried pace he ascends the steps of the furnace. He has nearly reached the top. He stops. Now the vast assembly eagerly listen for a royal address. But why turns he not his face toward the throng? Regardless of the swaying masses, he lifts his hand on high - he speaks! Hark! "Shadrach, Meshach, and Abednego, ye servants of the most high God, come forth and come hither!"

At the conclusion of this, which seemed to the multitude an incomprehensible speech, there were but few present who did not inwardly pronounce the king to be laboring under a sudden fit of insanity.

While all is still and solemn, behold, arm in arm, the forms of Shadrach, Meshach, and Abednego! A heavenly smile rests on their countenances. Already they have reached the top, and they stand in the presence of the wondering thousands. For a moment they cast a smiling glance on the throng below; then, with that ease of manner which always characterized them, they approach the king, and make their obeisance, with as much apparent good feeling as if nothing of an unkind nature had ever transpired. The king grasps them by the hand, and a mighty shout of good feeling and gladness resounds from thrice ten thousand tongues. The king then, turning to the multitude, in a loud voice exclaims:

"Blessed be the God of Shadrach, Meshach, and Abednego, who hath sent his angel and delivered his servants that trusted in him, and have yielded their bodies that they might not serve nor worship any god except their own God. Therefore I make a decree, that every people, nation, and language, which speak anything amiss against the God of Shadrach, Meshach, and Abednego, shall be cut in pieces; because there is no other god that can deliver after this sort. And now, by the command of the king, let that image be taken down, and let it be carried to the temple of Belus, and there, in a secluded part, let it remain."

The assembly was now disbanded and broken up by royal authority. The masses began to move homeward with deep astonishment. The golden image was lost sight of, and the miraculous deliverance of the three Hebrews was the all-absorbing theme. The priests of Belus were utterly confounded. This mighty demonstration of the power of Jehovah soon spread throughout the land. The numerous Hebrew captives were treated with much more kindness; thousands of Chaldeans lost all confidence in their gods, and learned to pay their homage at the shrine of Jehovah.

Daniel returned from the court of Pharaoh, after having arranged all things to the satisfaction of his sovereign, in whose estimation he now stood higher than ever. The three brothers were held in awe and reverence by all, and the king communed with them freely on all subjects. Their lives were rendered comfortable, and, according to the late decree of the king, whosoever dared to speak disrespectfully of their God did so at his imminent peril.

The priests of Belus kept much within their temple, and whenever they appeared in public, it was with far greater modesty and much less arrogance. They were fast losing the confidence of the populace, and the worship of the gods was greatly disregarded. The great Rab Mag was universally admired, and his three companions stood above reproach.

# CHAPTER XIX.

FOR some years after that wonderful display of Divine power, as exhibited before vast thousands on the plains of Dura, Chaldea was comparatively free from wars.

The king contented himself with adding to the already magnificent grandeur of the seat of his empire. Thousands were continually employed in carrying out the schemes developed by his inventive mind, and no sooner was one mighty enterprise completed, than another project was brought forward. But the monarch's vast ambition was not to be satisfied by the erection of massive walls and costly edifices. The fire of war and the love of conquest were not yet quenched in his soul. He had a strong passion for the din of battle.

Tyre was a strong and opulent city on the Mediterranean coast of Syria. It was one of the most celebrated maritime cities of antiquity, and remarkable for its power and grandeur. Hitherto, it had never been subject to any foreign power. It was built by the Sidonians, two hundred and forty years before the Temple of Jerusalem. For Sidon being taken by the Philistines of Askelon, many of its inhabitants made their escape in ships, and founded the city of Tyre; and for this reason we find it called in Isaiah, the "Daughter of Sidon." But the daughter soon surpassed the mother in grandeur, riches, and power.

Toward this proud city of Syria, the King of Babylon, in the twenty-first year of his reign, led his conquering legions, with full confidence of a speedy surrender. With a powerful army he encamped before the city, and soon commenced his attack, which was vigorously repelled. It became evident to the Chaldeans that the subduing of Tyre was not the work of a few days, or even a few months. His troops suffered incredible hardships, so that, according to the Prophet's expression, "every head was made bald, and every shoulder was peeled." Not until after a protracted siege of thirteen years was the city conquered, and even then Nebuchadnezzar found nothing to recompense him for the suffering of his army and the expense of the campaign.

Soon after the surrender of Tyre, the King of Babylon led his forces into Egypt, where he was much more successful than on the shores of the Mediterranean. A large number of provinces were brought to subjection, and thousands of captives were carried to Chaldea and distributed along the shores of the Euphrates.

The king of Babylon "was at rest in his own house, and flourishing in his own palace." The thoughts of the past, present, and future deeply occupied his mind. The past of his own history had been crowned with unparalleled success. The present was all that his heart could wish. He found himself surrounded with glory and magnificence that completely eclipsed the splendor of all other nations combined. The future - ah, the future! Who could penetrate its darkness? Could it be possible that the predictions of Belteshazzar, in regard to the future, were true? Was the glory of

Chaldea to be trampled in the dust? Was the kingly line of Nebuchadnezzar to be broken? Was not the kingdom at last established on an immovable foundation? But, had he not, at different times, been convinced that Belteshazzar had been instructed by the God of heaven in regard to the future? Tea, truly! But many years had passed since then, and his greatness had been daily increasing. The king would have gladly persuaded himself that all was clear in the future, but it was beyond his power, and under a degree of perplexity he threw himself upon his couch. A few wandering thoughts, and the king was asleep.

. . . . . . .

"Another dream of troubles!" cried the king, while his countenance bespoke alarm. "Do the gods, indeed, delight in my misery? Why must I be thus tormented? Aye! a dream big with meaning! A vision surcharged with great events! But who will show me the interpretation thereof? Where is Belteshazzar! But why may not my Chaldean wise men answer the purpose? Yea! Let them have the first trial. Why do I thus tremble? Whom shall I fear? 'Hew down the tree!' O, ye gods, how that voice sounded! 'Let his portion be with the beasts, in the grass of the earth!' What meaneth it? Why do I fear to call Belteshazzar first? Is it not best at once to know the worst? But let my Chaldeans have the first trial;" and the king called a young page into his presence.

"Young man, where is thy father?"

"My father is in the adjoining chamber, O king."

"Call him hither without delay."

The page hastened from the presence of the king, and presently a venerable-looking person walked into the apartment, and bowed in reverence before the king.

"Arioch, it is my desire to see the wise men of Babylon as soon as possible at this apartment. Go! Haste thee! for the command of the king is urgent. Let them be native Chaldeans who appear before me at this time; trouble not Belteshazzar. If I need his services I shall call for him hereafter."

The officer, faithful to his charge, was soon on his way to summon the wise men to appear before the king.

It was not long before a number of the Chaldeans stood in the presence of the king, ready to learn his will and do his pleasure.

"Are ye able to give me the correct interpretation of a wonderful dream?" asked the king, in a doubtful tone.

"We surely can, O king!" replied the chief of the wise men; "we derive our knowledge from the gods, and the interpretation of the dream must be sure."

"But what proof do your gods give of their own existence?" asked the king, looking sternly on the chief.

"Our gods made the world, O king!"

"Some gods, or God, made the world; but why not the God of Israel? Can you point to any miraculous interference of your gods in the affairs of mortals? If I have forgotten my dream, can ye, through your gods, restore it? And if, in case ye fail, I should cast you all into a fiery furnace, would your gods preserve you unhurt in the midst of the fire? Answer me!"

"Thy servants," said the trembling magician, "from their youth up have been taught to reverence and adore the gods of Chaldea. That there is a God in Israel, we are ready to admit; and far be it from us to hide from the king our convictions that this God has given us infallible proofs of his power. This we do not admit before the populace: but why should we dissemble before our king? Since the issuing of thy decree on the plains of Dura, we have never said aught against the God of the Hebrews. Let thy servants, I pray thee, find favor in thy sight, and deal not with us harshly!"

"At this time," said the king, "ye are not required to restore a lost dream. I have the vision in all its parts, and, if ye are able, ye may give me the interpretation. If ye are not able, confess your ignorance, or, by the God of Israel, I will pour my vengeance on every head!"

The king then carefully rehearsed his dream in their presence. When he had finished he arose, and, approaching the head magician, with a look that made him tremble, he asked:

"Canst thou or thy comrades give me the interpretation of this wonderful dream?"

"The king's dreams are at all times of a very peculiar nature, and far different from ordinary dreams," replied the prince of the magicians. "The king demands honesty at our hands, and may the gods forbid that we should be otherwise. We are not able to give thee the interpretation of thy wonderful dream. We fall on thy

·mercy! Oh, deal not harshly with thy servants!"

"Thy simple honesty hath at this time saved thy life and the lives of thy companions! Go your way, and bear in mind that ye are a band of hypocritical pretenders. I have demanded your service for the last time!"

The magicians hurried away from the palace, thankful that they had escaped so well; and nevermore were their services required in the presence of the king.

"Much as I expected! The vile, deceitful race! The gods! Much they know about the gods. Have we any gods? I have no proof of any god but the God of the Hebrews. Belteshazzar must at last explain the vision! Why do I dread the knowledge of it? Is this trembling the result of fear? The day is damp and cold. 'Hew down the tree!' That voice was solemn! Why must I remain in this suspense? I will know the worst! If the God of the Hebrews has a quarrel with the King of Babylon, let me know it! Without delay I'll send for Belteshazzar."

The prime minister, always obedient to the demands of his sovereign, hastened into the presence of Nebuch-adnezzar, where he was received with the most profound respect.

"O Belteshazzar, master of the magicians, because I know that the spirit of the holy gods is in thee, and no secret troubleth thee, tell me the visions of my dream that I have seen, and the interpretation thereof. Thus were the visions of my head on my bed: I saw a tree in the midst of the earth, and the height thereof was great. The tree grew, and was strong, and the height thereof reached unto heaven, and the sight thereof to the end of all the earth; the leaves thereof were fair, and the fruit thereof much, and in it was meat for all; the beasts of the field had shadow under it, and the fowls of the heaven dwelt in the boughs thereof, and all flesh was fed of it. I saw in the vision of my head upon my bed, and behold a watcher, and a holy one came down from heaven! He cried aloud, and said thus, 'Hew down the tree and cut off his branches, shake off his leaves, and scatter his fruit; let the beasts get away from under it, and the fowls from his branches. Nevertheless, leave the stump of his roots in the earth, even with a band of iron and brass in the tender grass of the field; and let it be wet with the dew of heaven, and let his portion be with the beasts in the grass of the earth. Let his heart be changed from man's, and let a beast's heart be given unto him; and let seven times pass over him. This matter is by the decree of the watchers, and the demand by the word of the holy ones, to the intent that the living may know that the Most High ruleth in the kingdom of men, and giveth to whomsoever he will, and setteth up over it the basest of men.' This dream I, King Nebuchadnezzar, have seen. Now thou, O Belteshazzar, declare the interpretation thereof, forasmuch as all the wise men of my kingdom are not able to make known unto me the interpretation; but thou art able, for the spirit of the holy gods is in thee."

Daniel was astonished, and his thoughts greatly troubled him.

"Belteshazzar," said the king, "let not the dream or the interpretation thereof give thee pain or uneasiness."

"My lord," said Daniel, "the dream is to them that hate thee, and the interpretation thereof to thine enemies.

The tree that thou sawest, which grew and was strong, whose height reached into the heavens, and the sight thereof to all the earth, it is thou, O king, that art grown and become strong; for thy greatness is grown and reacheth unto heaven, and thy dominion to the end of the earth. And whereas the king saw a watcher and a holy one coming down from heaven, and saying, 'Hew down the tree and destroy it, yet leave the stump of the roots thereof in the earth, even with the band of iron and brass in the tender grass of the field, and let it be wet with the dew of heaven, and let his portion be with the beasts of the field till seven times pass over him,' this is the interpretation, O king, and this is the decree of the Most High which is come upon my lord the king: that they shall drive thee from men, and thy dwelling shall be with the beasts of the field, and they shall make thee eat grass as oxen, and they shall wet thee with the dew of heaven; and seven times shall pass over thee, till thou know that the Most High ruleth in the kingdom of men, and giveth to whomsoever he will. And whereas they commanded to leave the stump of the tree roots, thy kingdom shall be sure unto thee, after that thou shalt have known that the heavens do rule. Wherefore, O king, let my counsel be acceptable to thee, and break off thy sins by righteousness, and thine iniquities by showing mercy to the poor, if it may be a lengthening of thy tranquility."

The king, conscious that the Hebrew was under peculiar inspiration, bowed in solemn reverence, dismissed him in the most respectful manner, and then threw himself on his couch, in the deepest agony of mind.

"The fates are against me! What shall I do? Shall I weep like a woman, and sob like a corrected child?

Shall the King of Babylon, the great conqueror of nations, turn at last to be a coward? Shall the great sovereign of Chaldea say he is sorry, beg pardon of the gods, and thus reduce himself to the level of a common subject? Never! Let all the gods hear it! Never! 'Driven from among men!' Who shall be able to drive Nebuchadnezzar? 'Eat grass as oxen!' O, ye gods, is not that laughable? And yet I cannot laugh! Let it come! I fear not the gods! Ah, do I not? I fear not the gods, but still I have a dread of that one God. I destroyed his temple, I plundered his sanctuary, I carried his vessels to the house of my god, in the land of Shinar. Is he about to retaliate? I shall see. Shall I humble myself before a strange god? Shall I now, after having reached the very pinnacle of fame and glory, dishonor myself in the eyes of my nobles? Nay! Sooner than this, I will brave the vengeance of all the gods and nobly perish in the unequal conflict!"

. . . . . . .

Twelve months passed after the King of Babylon was troubled by his wonderful dream. His grief was not of long duration, and this period had been one of more than usual gayety and hilarity in the great city. The king gave entertainments on a magnificent scale; and, in the midst of his dazzling splendor, the mournful predictions of Belteshazzar were well-nigh forgotten. Occasionally they would rush to the monarch's mind, but with a desperate effort they would be banished as troublesome intruders and unwelcome guests.

. . . . . . .

The day was beautifully clear. The king, about the ninth hour of the day, walked upon the roof of his high palace. Babylon, in all its glory, stood before him, its massive walls bidding defiance to all the surrounding nations. The temple of Belus, with its famous tower, stood forth in majestic grandeur, together with the hanging gardens, decorated with all that was beautiful and lovely in nature. The city's famous buildings he could count by thousands, and its rich palaces by tens of thousands. The predictions of Daniel found way to the monarch's mind; but they were expelled by a proud spirit and stubborn will. His soul laughed to scorn the dark prophecy.

"What!" said the proud monarch, "does this look like 'eating grass like an ox'? Is not this great Babylon, that I have built for the house of the kingdom by the might of my power, and for the honor of my majesty? Who shall - " Hark! A voice speaks from the heavens! "O King Nebuchadnezzar, to thee it is spoken: The kingdom is departed from thee, and they shall drive thee from among men; and thy dwelling shall be with the beasts of the field; they shall make thee eat grass as oxen; and seven times shall pass over thee, until thou knowest that the Most High ruleth in the kingdom of men."

The voice ceased. The king uttered a loud, hysterical laugh, descended from his palace, and ran into the park, a raving maniac.

. . . . . ..

Stillness reigns in the home of Joram. No merry voices fall on the ear of the passer-by. The few that move around the premises tread carefully and silently, while solemnity settles on each countenance. The voice of song is hushed; the loud peals of melody are no longer heard; and for many a day the "Harp of Judah" has remained in its corner, and no delicate hand has swept its well-tuned strings. Inside of that mansion to-day you witness not that joy which is wont to pervade it. You perceive cheeks wet with tears, and bosoms heaving with sighs. The inmates converse together in whispers, and tread lightly. In an apartment richly furnished, into which the beams of the sun are not permitted to enter, we find assembled a large company of relatives and near friends. It is not an occasion of small import that calls them thus together. There we find Mathias, Perreeza, and their children. The amiable Jupheena is there, with her husband and sons and daughters. Venerable men and women are seen here and there.

But where to-night is Joram? Where is that benign countenance? Hush! Speak low, tread lightly! Disturb not the last moments of the dying Israelite! Joram is at the banks of Jordan. Already his feet are touching the cold waters.

The sick man turns on his pillow and faintly

"Mathias, why comes he not? Shall I not once more see my most excellent friend?"

"My dear father, he will ere long be here. The messenger is trustworthy, and will soon return."

"The journey of life is near its close. The holy hill is in sight. I pass through the vale of death on my way to the better land. Yonder is the home of the faithful. Sorrow and mourning shall flee away."

"He is here! He is here!" cried Jupheena.

"Has he arrived?" asked the sick man, in faint accents.

"Yea, father," replied Mathias, in soothing tones, "he has arrived."

"Thanks be to Jehovah!"

Presently, a man of venerable appearance, his hair silvered over with age, apparently a Chaldean, walked into the apartment. Jupheena was the first to greet him.

"Jehovah bless my lovely daughter!" whispered the aged man, as the tears coursed down his furrowed cheeks. For a moment he looked around upon the company with an earnestness of affection not easily described; then looking up to heaven, in trembling accents he broke forth:

"Oh, Jehovah, let the smiles of Thy countenance rest on these Thy chosen ones!"

The venerable man was then gently led by Mathias to the bedside.

A smile passed over the pale countenance of Joram, the fountain of his tears overflowed; he looked up to the face of his old friend, reached out his trembling hand, and cried:

"Ah! my good Barzello! thou hast come once more to see thy friend Joram, before he leaves for the spirit land."

"If thou art to go first," replied the old soldier, "we shall not long be separated; with me, also, the battle of life will soon be closed."

"I find, Barzello, that my race is well-nigh run! I am fast passing away. I have a strong impression that this day I shall join the society of immortals; therefore I thought fit to send for my best friend, to be with me in my dying moments. I am spared to see a good old age. For the last forty years my cup of joy has been often filled and running over. Jehovah has dealt with his servant in great kindness. The iniquities of my youth are forgiven - I am at peace with the God of Israel."

The sick man desired to be raised a little higher on his pillow.

"That is better. Now I can see you all. We must soon part; my sun is fast sinking, and in a few hours Joram will be gone. The chariot will soon call. I chide you not for your tears, for here on earth I know too well their value. In that bright world above where Jehovah dwells, and where angels spread their wings, no tears are found."

Joram, quite exhausted, closed his eyes, and deep silence for a while prevailed. He soon revived, and called for Perreeza.

"What can I do for my ever-dear uncle?" whispered Perreeza.

"One more little song, accompanied by the harp of Judah," said Joram, with a smile, "and I ask no more."

"Perreeza greatly fears that it will disturb thee."

"Nay, my sweet child, thy Uncle Esrom was never yet disturbed by the sound of melody. Sing to me that little song thy aunt so dearly loved."

"Oh, my dear uncle," whispered the weeping Perreeza, "I fear it is beyond my power to sing. I am filled with weeping. Yet, at thy request, I will make the effort. Oh, God of my fathers, help me!"

"He will, my child," faintly answered the old Israelite; "get thy harp and sing."

Once again the old harp was brought from its corner. Perreeza wiped away her tears, and succeeded in conquering her emotions. She took the familiar instrument in her arms, and sat at a little distance from the dying man. Joram cast one look on the old harp, smiled, and gently closed his eyes. Perreeza softly touched the chords and sang:

> *"Father, send Thy heavenly chariot,*
> *Call Thy weeping child away;*
> *Long I've waited for Thy coming,*
> *Why, O why, this long delay?*
> *Of this earth my soul is weary,*
> *Yonder lies the better land;*
> *Fain my soul would leave its prison,*
> *Glad to join the glorious band.*
>
> *"Thrice ten thousand happy spirits*
> *Sing Thy praise in heaven above;*
> *All arrayed in robes of glory.*
> *Crowned with righteousness and love;*
> *Old companions wait to greet me,*
> *Smilingly they bid me come.*
> *Father, send Thy heavenly chariot,*
> *Call Thy weary pilgrim home.*
>
> *"Earth is fading from my vision;*
> *Brightness gathers o'er my head:*

*Thrilling strains from heavenly harpers*
*Sound around my dying bed.*
*Blessed land of saints and angels!*
*Here I can no longer stay;*
*Yonder comes my Father's chariot;*
*Rise, my soul, and haste away!"*

The song was ended. The harp was laid aside.

"Did my father enjoy the song?" soothingly inquired Mathias. Joram made no reply. The "chariot" had arrived, and Joram had departed! As the last vibrations of the "harp of Judah" died on the ear, his soul was wafted on angelic pinions, and introduced to the melody around the throne of God.

# CHAPTER XX.

AFTER the insanity of Nebuchadnezzar, Evil-Merodach, his son, acted as regent. The misfortune of the Chaldean monarch cast a deep gloom over the vast empire. He fell at the zenith of his popularity, and the government throughout felt the shock. Evil-Merodach was far from being a favorite, and among all classes in the nation there seemed to be a growing dissatisfaction. This feeling would have been immeasurably greater had it not been for the wisdom and vigilance of Belteshazzar, his prime minister. Of Daniel's wisdom the regent had no doubt. From his father he had learned all the particulars in regard to Daniel's interpretation of the dream; and, seeing before his eyes daily a literal fulfillment of its awful predictions, he could not but hold the interpreter in much reverence.

Nearly seven years passed without witnessing events of special importance in the empire. During most of this time Nebuchadnezzar exhibited all the signs of a maniac. As he showed no disposition to injure those around him, he was permitted to go at large, within royal inclosures. His treatment was much according to the direction of Daniel, who was the only person at the palace of whom the maniac king appeared to have the least recognition. He carefully shunned the presence of every one, and the only thing that appeared to give him satisfaction and check his raving was the permission to be a companion of his oxen, that quietly fed in the palace park. Here it may be well to remark that the peculiar feature of the king's insanity was the strange conviction that he was an ox; and, under this conviction, he would endeavor to imitate that animal in all its motions and voices. He was never confined or bound with chains, but permitted to enjoy himself as his maniac fancies might dictate. This was not the result of indifference, but quite the contrary. The king was held in much respect at the palace, even in his deplorable insanity; and there was much faith placed in the opinion of Daniel in regard to the king's final restoration to his reason and the kingdom. Among many of Daniel's Chaldean friends at the court the opinion was becoming prevalent that the interesting occasion was not far distant.

. . . . . . .

The afternoon was fair and beautiful. It was about the ninth hour of the day. Daniel, weary with his arduous duties within, thought fit, in order to invigorate both his body and mind, to take a walk in the beautiful groves of the palace park. So he laid his papers aside, and was soon under the refreshing breezes of the open skies. The scene was truly delightful. The sun was gradually losing the intensity of its heat, and slowly sinking toward the western hills. Nature was adorned in beauty and innocence. The sweet choristers of the trees chanted their melodious sonnets on the high branches, and the parks rang with the sound of praise from the feathered tribe. The river rolled majestically along, while its shores were strewed with the choicest roses and flowers. On the banks of "proud Euphrates' stream," the Rab Mag sat down and gave freedom to his thoughts.

"His paths are unsearchable, and His ways past finding out! He reigns in heaven above, and on earth beneath. Jehovah is God alone. By him kings rule and princes govern. He taketh down one and setteth up another. O Lord, thou art very great, and highly exalted above all gods. In thy hands are the deep places of the earth: the strength of the hills is thine also. I adore thee, O my God! I praise thee, O Jehovah! From my youth the God of Israel has been my help. He has brought me through ways I have not known. How terrible is his wrath toward those who rebel against him! How great his love to all that fear him! He bringeth down the proud look, and causeth his enemies to be ashamed. The scepters of kings are broken in pieces. Jehovah is King of kings! Babylon, with all her glory, shall become a desolation. Her lofty towers shall fall, her walls shall be destroyed, her palaces shall become heaps of ruin, and her idol temples shall be no more!"

Such were the meditations of Daniel, when his attention was called to a rustling noise in the foliage, on his right, a short distance from the spot on which he sat. He looked, and beheld the uncouth form of the maniac king slowly approaching him. The sight affected the Hebrew's heart. His eyes became moistened with tears. The punishment was just, he knew; but in the history of that degraded monarch, he could find many things to admire. In other days he had a heart that throbbed with kind and warm emotions. Had he not in the main been kind to him and his three companions? And, in the midst of envy and jealousy, had he not kept them, foreigners as they were, in the highest offices in the gift of the government? He had. And Daniel's heart throbbed with pity as he beheld the brutish antics of one who was once so powerful and intelligent. The king gradually approached the spot where Daniel sat, without observing him, sometimes standing erect, other times running on all fours, sometimes uttering incoherent expressions, other times bellowing like an ox.

"God of my fathers," silently cried Daniel, "let this suffice! According to thy promise restore the unhappy king to his reason, and let his courtiers know that there is no God like unto thee."

By this time the maniac stood close by the side of his courtier, but as yet he had not observed him.

"Nebuchadnezzar, king of Babylon!" cried Daniel, with a loud voice.

The maniac was startled, looked up to the face of the minister for a moment, and cried, in loud accents, "Belteshazzar! Belteshazzar!" and, as if greatly terrified, ran. He soon stopped and stood at a distance, with his wild, flashing eyes steadfastly fixed on the form of the Rab Mag.

Daniel arose, and slowly directed his footsteps towards the spot. He was glad to find that the king remained stationary. He approached within a respectful distance of the maniac, uncovered his head, made his humble obeisance as in days of yore, and cried:

"O king, live forever!"

The king, in silence, continued to gaze on Daniel, with a wild, vacant stare.

"Jehovah, the God of Israel!" cried Daniel, pointing with his finger to the skies.

"J-e-h-o-v-a-h!" slowly whispered the king, gazing upward.

The Hebrew now ventured nearer the king, fell upon his knees, and "with his face toward Jerusalem," sent his urgent, silent petition to the God of Israel, in behalf of his unfortunate sovereign. Daniel had not been long in prayer before the king, with restored reason, fell down by his side and loudly rejoiced and praised the God of heaven. The set time had come; the prayer of the man of God had, indeed, prevailed; the lost was found, the maniac was restored.

The restoration of reason to the king was brought about by the same miraculous power that had deprived him of it, and it was accomplished in the same sudden manner. He was not only restored to the right use of his faculties, but also to a perfect recollection of the past. The dream, its interpretation, with all subsequent transactions up to the very day of his insanity, were brought clearly to his mind; but since that moment all was one dark void. In mercy, not a vestige was permitted to remain to embitter his after years.

The most important thing that now appeared to occupy the monarch's mind was the life and health of his family, and the length of the period of his insanity.

"Tell me, O Belteshazzar, how long has the king of Babylon remained in this degraded condition?"

"Seven years of deep calamity, O king, have passed over thy head!"

"Seven years!" cried the king, with a trembling voice, while his tears were fast falling. "O thou God of heaven, thou art just in all thy ways! But are the members of my family spared to see the restoration of the king?"

"They are all spared and in good health, O king, and will be overjoyed to see thee restored to thy throne."

"Jehovah is the only God! He ruleth among the armies of the heavens, and the inhabitants of the earth. Let all nations praise the God of Israel! But come, Belteshazzar, let us bend our footsteps towards the palace."

Daniel threw one of his loose garments over the almost naked form of the king, side by side, they started towards the palace royal. On their way thither, they were met by the captain of the guard. The old soldier was overwhelmed with joy to hear once more the familiar voice of his beloved king. He fell before him, and would have embraced his feet if permitted. He begged of the king to remain where he was with Belteshazzar, and permit him to hasten to the palace to herald the joyful news, and return with the king's old guard to escort him home. The measure struck the king favorably, and Arioch, with a bounding heart, was on his way. The regent, Evil-Merodach, was first apprised of the fact, which he received with demonstrations of joy.

The news was quickly learned by hundreds, and the palace rang with shouts of rejoicing. The regent, with the guard, was soon on the march for the place where Arioch had left the king. When they reached the spot, the monarch arose and gently bowed. His son now ran up to his father, fell on his neck, and they warmly embraced each other. The old royal guard, as soon as their emotions were partially subsided, approached as near their sovereign as they could, and, at a given signal from their captain, they broke forth in one grand shout that made the forest ring. The king was deeply moved; he endeavored to speak, but was not able.

The procession was on its way. The king with his son and the prime minister, was drawn in the royal chariot. Shouts of joy echoed on the high turrets of the royal mansion as the restored monarch entered once more through its massive portals, to sit on the throne of his empire. Heralds were hurried into every part of the city to acquaint officials with the king's restoration, and on that night the great metropolis of Chaldea was brilliantly illuminated, and loud shouts of rejoicing burst forth from thousands of gladdened hearts.

The king resumed the responsible duties of his government amid the warm congratulations and the best wishes of his courtiers and subjects. New life was infused into every department of state, and the metropolis once more appeared to breathe the breath of former years.

Belteshazzar was now to the king a constant and confiding friend. They conversed together freely on all points, and no measure was put forth without the consent and approbation of the Rab Mag.

In regard to the God of Israel no doubt remained longer in the mind of the king. At last he was wholly saved from idolatry. The process of his conversion had been a severe one, but in the hands of Jehovah it had proved successful. His vanity was conquered, his haughtiness slain, the pride of his heart subdued; he was a meek and lowly worshiper at the shrine of the

God of Israel.

The king was getting well stricken in years, and he was conscious that he was not long for earth. Therefore, like a wise man, he bestowed much thought on that world into which he was fast hastening. His worldly ambition was at an end, he appeared but seldom in public, and was much given to retirement and meditation. He had at last learned to see the things of earth in their true light, and the enthusiasm of his younger friends was viewed with a smile and a sigh. He clearly saw in the distance the glory of Babylon brought to the dust, and its majestic halls resounding with the voice of revelry from the sons and daughters of strangers. Of this the reformed king could not think without painful emotions; but with resignation he bowed to the Will divine.

# CHAPTER XXI.

ON THE death of Nebuchadnezzar, Evil-Merodach took the throne. Of this man we have said but little. He acted as regent during his father's Insanity. He was a person of a low, groveling mind, and no sooner was he established on his throne than he began to give signs that the scepter was in the hands of a profligate tyrant. Contrary to the request of his dying father, he neglected the weighty matters of the empire, and plunged into dissipation and gluttonous revelry.

As with the commencement of Nebuchadnezzar's reign began the real glory of Chaldea, so with his death the glory departed, and the empire was soon in a rapid decline. No feature in the character of the new king was in the least calculated to command either the love or the admiration of his subjects. He was inwardly cursed by the nation, and feared only on account of his cruelty. Of Daniel he had some dread, and over him the Hebrew had some control. He was well convinced, from what he had seen in his father's history, that Daniel was not to be slighted, and that among all the wise men of the realm, there was none like him. And, moreover, he was well aware that his superior wisdom had had much to do in elevating the empire to its present high position. Through the influence of this man of God, the wicked king dealt with comparative mildness toward the captive Hebrews so  numerous

Erasmus W. Jones

within the realm.

The reign of this monarch was of short duration. Some of his own relatives, conspiring against him, put an end to his existence; and so died Evil-Merodach, unwept by the nation, and Nerriglisser, one of the chief conspirators, reigned in his stead.

The three brothers, since the death of Nebuchadnezzar, had seen best to retire from public life. In Babylon they were greatly beloved, and considered as the peculiarly favored of the gods, and over whom no mortal had control.

Nerriglisser, immediately on his accession to the throne, made great preparations for war against the Medes, which preparations lasted for three years. Cyaxeres, king of the Medes, seeing the hostile attitude of the Babylonians, sent to Persia, imploring the help of his young nephew, Cyrus, the son of Cambyses, king of Persia, who had married his sister Mandana. Now Cyrus was beautiful in person, and still more lovely in the qualities of his mind; was of sweet disposition, full of good nature and humanity, and always had a great desire to learn and a noble ardor for glory. He was never afraid of danger nor discouraged by any hardship or difficulty. He was brought up according to the laws and customs of the Persians, which were excellent in those days with respect to education. With the consent of his father, he readily complied with the wish of his uncle, and, at the head of 30,000 well-trained Persians, he marched into Media and thence to Assyria, to meet the forces of Nerriglisser, king of Babylon, and the forces of Croesus, king of the Lydians. The armies met. The Chaldeans were routed. Croesus fled, and Nerriglisser, the king of Babylon, was slain in the action. His son, Loboros-barchod, succeeded to the throne.

This was a very wicked prince. Being naturally of the most vicious inclinations, he now indulged them without restraint, as if he had been invested with sovereign power only to have the privilege of committing with impunity the most infamous and barbarous actions. He reigned but five months; his own subjects, conspiring against him, put him to death, and Belshazzar, the son of Evil-Merodach, reigned in his place.

Since the death of Evil-Merodach, and during the reign of his two successors, Daniel had retired to private life, and was but little spoken of at public places. This king, following in the footsteps of his predecessors, led a life of dissipation and profligacy.

In the meantime, the fame of the Persian prince was spreading far and wide. His armies proved victorious on every shore; and, to the faithful Hebrews, who discerned the signs of the times, his conquests were hailed with inward joy. Cyrus for some years had tarried in Asia Minor, and had reduced all the nations that inhabited it to subjection, from the Aegean Sea to the River Euphrates. Then he proceeded to Syria and Arabia, which he also subdued.

The fortifications of Babylon, since the death of Nebuchadnezzar, had been strengthened, and now the work of fortifying was carried on with great vigor. Belshazzar, if from no other motive than fear, gave all encouragement to this kind of improvement, and during his reign prodigious works of this nature were completed. He was well aware that the famous Persian had his eye upon him, and that the besieging of the city was but a question of time. He therefore made all preparations for a formidable attack. Provisions of all kinds, from all parts of the country, were stored within the city in great abundance, and everything was put in readiness to withstand a protracted siege.

Cyrus, whom divine Providence was to make use of, was mentioned in the Scriptures by his name one hundred and fifty years before he was born in these words:

"Thus saith the Lord to his anointed, to Cyrus, whose right hand I have holden, to subdue nations before him; and I will loose the loins of kings, to open before him the two-leaved gates; and the gates shall not be shut. I will go before thee and make the crooked places straight; I will break in pieces the gates of brass, and cut in sunder the bars of iron; and I will give thee the treasures of darkness and hidden riches of secret places; that thou mayest know that I, the Lord, which call thee by thy name, am the God of Israel. For Jacob my servant's sake, and Israel mine elect, I have even called thee by thy name: I have surnamed thee, though thou hast not known me" (Isa. 45: 1-4).

# CHAPTER XXII.

THE army of Cyrus had already reached the capital of Chaldea. The vast plain before the city swarmed with moving thousands of Medes and Persians. At this time no warriors were finer in appearance than the battlemen of the Persian prince. Their discipline had reached to an almost inconceivable degree of perfection. The wishes and desires of their great commander had become their law; and each one vied with the other in rendering obedience to his orders. Their fame had spread throughout lower Asia, and through many parts of Assyria.

But the Babylonians thought themselves so well prepared for this emergency that the numerous legions of Cyrus failed to alarm them. Their walls they considered proof against any attack, and they had a sufficient amount of provision in the city for twenty years. They laughed to scorn the demand of the Persians, and loudly ridiculed them from the city walls. Belshazzar and his counselors, considering themselves secure, gave way to their depraved appetites. The palace was one scene of debauchery and revelry by day and by night.

The Persian general soon saw that an assault on such formidable defenses would be useless. A project was conceived in his mind. He made the inhabitants believe that he intended to reduce the city by famine. To this end he caused a line of circumvallation to be drawn quite around the city with a large and deep ditch; and, that his troops might not be over-fatigued, he divided his army into twelve bodies, and assigned to each of them its month of guarding the trenches. The great ditch was completed, but the reveling Babylonians little thought of its real design.

Belshazzar, the king, made a feast to a thousand of his lords, and drank wine before the thousand. This feast was one of great splendor. The most spacious and magnificent rooms in the richest city in the world were crowded with rank and beauty. Learning, aristocracy and royalty were there. Precious stones and costly perfumery filled the salon with dazzling luster and sweet fragrance. Wit sparkled with the sparkling of the cups, and reason flowed with the flowing of the wine. They drank toasts of enthusiastic patriotism; they sang songs of unbounded loyalty, and shouted defiance to every foe. Strains of melody poured forth from an hundred instruments, and hilarity and excessive mirth beamed forth from every countenance. The high praises of the gods of Chaldea, with rapturous shouts in honor to their king, mingled together and broke forth from a thousand tongues. The besieging army and its commander, together with the God of the Hebrews, were made the subjects of their keenest sarcasm.

This feast was given in honor of Belshazzar's birth; and we may easily judge that flattery without measure was poured into his willing ear. On this occasion, from the very nature of the festival, much was expected from the monarch himself, and it was very evident that he was fully determined that in this they should not be disappointed. He spoke in this vein:

"All hail, brave Babylonians! Welcome! Thrice welcome to the presence of your king! Before me on this night I behold the pride and glory of Babylon. Here are my nobles who have at all times distinguished themselves by their valor and great bravery. Let us banish gloom, and let our hearts overflow with mirth! We may well congratulate ourselves on the perfect safety of Babylon. Our walls are impregnable and our possessions are abundant. We laugh to scorn the silly movements of the Persians that parade before the city. Dark predictions there are, I know, in regard to the future of Chaldea, but these Hebrew delusions have well-nigh vanished. I am sorry to confess that my royal grandsire gave too much countenance to these ground-less delusions, in the preferment of the Hebrew Belteshazzar with his three companions to high offices within the province of Babylon. This, my lords, was a great mistake of the past, for which we have already too dearly paid. Since I came to the throne, this intermeddling of foreigners with the affairs of the nation has received no countenance; and happy am I to know that to-day all offices under the government are entrusted to none but native Chaldeans. In this I do not wish to cast a shade on the memories of the illustrious dead, for truly no monarch ever distinguished himself more than my lamented grandfather. The trophies of his victories are to-day visible throughout the empire. To him, indeed, the gods of Chaldea were propitious, and unmistakable proof they gave of their superiority to the gods of other nations. We have heard much of the renowned God of the Hebrews! But, under the protection of our own, we bid defiance to all other gods! Who is the God of Israel that I should fear him? Did not my grandfather, under the guidance of the gods of Chaldea, enter into his territory, destroy his city and burn his temple? Why did he not then vindicate his power and glory? Why permit the vessels of his temple to be carried into Babylon, and there deposited in the temple of Belus? Ah, my lords, those vessels were worthy of a more trusty god! They are beautiful to behold, and would well become an occasion like the present. Surely this is well thought! Let the vessels of the temple of the God of Israel be brought hither, and from them let us drink wine in honor of the gods of Chaldea! Bring them hither in haste! My thirst increases with the thought! All praise to our matchless gods! Again I say, let us banish gloom, and let us be filled with mirth! But here, indeed, come the temple vessels of the God of Israel! Bring them hither. Look ye here, Babylonians! Saw ye ever anything more beautiful? Such fine specimens of art as these must be rendered serviceable in the employ of more worthy gods! Let them be filled with wine! Let us drink to the gods of the empire; and, if there is a God in Israel, let him come to the rescue! We defy his power, Chaldeans! These Hebrews among us must be limited in their privileges. The worship of their imaginary God, if at all permitted, must be on a more private scale. They are corrupting in their influence, and their liberties must be restricted. This I have accomplished in a measure, and, by the gods, I swear that in this my pleasure must be realized to the full! These foreigners have too long lived in ease, and many of them have been unwisely elevated to fill the most responsible offices in the gift of the government, to the exclusion of Chaldeans and more worthy men. Of this We shall hear no more complaint. I have cut short the work, and not one Hebrew remains in office within the empire. Babylonians, in this has not the king met your wishes? Your joyous looks and merry countenances answer 'yea!' Let this then be our motto, 'Chaldeans to rule Chaldea!' Drink! Drink freely! Drink to the gods!

Is there a God in Israel? Let him come and claim the vessels of his sanctuary! Oh, the wine tastes delicious from these thy golden goblets! Oh, thou God of Israel! Ha! ha! ha! More wine! Let us rejoice and be glad, and drink defiance to all gods save the gods of Chaldea! Who shall Belshazzar fear? What god can alarm the king of Bab - "

The vessel fell from the monarch's hand! Paleness gathered on his brow! A sudden trembling shook his whole frame! A cry of terror broke from his lips!

On the wall, over against the candlestick, there appeared the fingers of a man's hand, which wrote on the plaster. This was the mysterious sight that gave terror to the king and alarmed the merry throng.

"Haste ye!" cried the terrified king, "and bring hither my wise men, and let them give me the signification of the writing. Go in haste!"

Messengers were speedily hurried to summon the magicians and wise men into the presence of the monarch, and within a short period the whole "college" stood before the agitated sovereign in the midst of the banqueting hall.

"Look ye yonder!" said the king, with a trembling voice, pointing to the mysterious writing. "Whosoever shall read this writing, and show me the interpretation thereof, shall be clothed with scarlet and have a chain of gold about his neck, and shall be the third ruler in the kingdom."

The wise men gazed in silent astonishment on the writing, cast solemn glances at one another, and at last frankly confessed that it was written in a language with which they had no acquaintance - peradventure, understood only by the gods.

"What shall I do?" cried the king, in deep agony. "I fear some awful calamity is about to befall me! A curse upon you pretenders' Depart from my presence! O ye gods, what shall I do?"

The great fear of the king had been made known to the queen-mother, the famous Nitocris, wife of Nebuchadnezzar. She hastened to the banquet chamber, where she found all in the greatest consternation, especially the king.

"O king, live forever!" cried the queen-mother. "Let not thy thoughts trouble thee, nor thy countenance thus be changed in the presence of thy mighty lords, lest hereafter they despise thy fear. There is a man in thy kingdom in whom is the spirit of the holy gods; and, in the days of thy grandfather, light and understanding and wisdom, like the wisdom of the gods, were found in him, whom the king, Nebuchadnezzar, thy grandfather - I say the king himself - made master of the magicians, astrologers and soothsayers; and this was a sure sign of his superior wisdom. This great man is not found among thy nobles. Since in thy great wisdom thou didst see fit to deprive all Hebrews of office, this mighty Daniel, whom thy grandfather called Belteshazzar, has been seen but seldom. But be it known to thee, O king, that he is not utterly forgotten."

Without delay messengers were sent to the house of Daniel, and in a short time a venerable person, with his hair silvered over, slowly marched into the banqueting hall, and, without the least embarrassment, stood in the presence of the pale and trembling Belshazzar.

"Art thou that Daniel who art of the captivity of Judah, whom the king my grandfather brought from Judah? I have even heard of thee that the spirit of the gods is in thee, and that light and understanding and excellence are found in thee. And now the wise men, the astrologers, have been brought in before me, that they should read this writing and make known unto me the interpretation thereof; but they could not show the interpretation of the thing. Now, if thou canst read the writing and make known to me the interpretation thereof, thou shalt be clothed with scarlet, and have a chain of gold about thy neck, and shall be the third ruler in the kingdom."

Then Daniel answered and said before the king:

"Let thy gifts be to thyself, and give thy rewards to another. Yet I will read the writing to the king, and make known unto him the interpretation.

"O thou king! the Most High God gave Nebuchadnezzar a kingdom, and majesty, and glory, and honor. All people, nations and languages trembled and feared before him. Whom he would he slew, and whom he would he kept alive; whom he would he set up, and whom he would he put down. But when his heart was lifted up, and his mind hardened in pride, he was deposed from his kingly throne and his glory was taken from him; and he was driven from the sons of men, and his heart was made like the beasts, and his dwelling was with the wild asses. They fed him with grass like oxen, and his body was wet with the dew of heaven, till he knew that the Most High God ruleth in the kingdom of men, and that he appointeth over it whomsoever he will. And thou, O Belshazzar, hast not humbled thy heart, though thou knewest all this, but hast lifted up thyself against the Lord of heaven; and they have brought the vessels of his house before thee, and thou and thy lords, thy wives and thy concubines, have drunk wine in them; and thou hast praised the gods of silver and gold, of brass, iron, wood and stone, which see not, nor bear, nor know; and the God in whose hand thy breath is, thou hast not glorified.

"This is the interpretation of the thing. Mene - God hath numbered thy kingdom and finished it; Tekel - thou art weighed in the balances and found wanting; Peres - thy kingdom is divided and given to the Medes and Persians."

Then commanded Belshazzar, and they clothed Daniel with scarlet, and put a chain of gold about his neck, and made a proclamation concerning him, that he should be the third ruler in the kingdom.

. . . . . . .

As soon as Cyrus saw that the ditches, which they had long worked upon, were finished, he began to plan for the execution of his vast design, which as yet he had communicated to no one. He was informed that, in the city, on a certain day, a great festival was to be celebrated, and that the Babylonians, on occasions of that solemnity, were accustomed to pass the whole night in drunkenness and debauchery. Of this impious feast we have already spoken. Thus Providence furnished him with as fit an opportunity as he could desire. He therefore posted a part of his troops on that side where the river entered the city, and another part on that side where it went out, and commanded them to enter the city that very night by marching along the channel of the river as soon as ever they found it fordable. Having given all necessary orders, he exhorted his officers to follow him - that he was under the direction of the gods. In the evening he gave orders to open the great receptacles, or ditches, on both sides of the town, above and below, that the waters of the rivers might run into them. By this means the Euphrates was quickly emptied and its channel became dry. Then the two bodies of troops, according to their orders, went into the channels, the one commanded by Gobryas and the other by Gadates, and advanced toward each other without meeting any impediment.

Thus did these two bodies of troops penetrate into the very heart of the city without opposition. According to agreement, they met together at the royal palace, surprised the guard, and slew them. The company, hearing the tumult without, opened the door. The Persian soldiers rushed in. They were met by the king with his sword in hand. He was slain, and hundreds of his drunken associates shared the same fate. Thus terminated the great banquet of Belshazzar, where the God of heaven was wickedly blasphemed; and thus terminated the Babylonian empire, after a duration of two hundred and ten years from the first of Nabonassar's reign, who was the founder thereof.

# CHAPTER XXIII.

IMMEDIATELY after the taking of Babylon, Cyrus ordered a day of public thanksgiving to the gods, for their wonderful favors and their kind interposition; and then, having assembled his principal officers, he publicly applauded their courage and prudence, their zeal and attachment to his person, and distributed rewards to his whole army. He also reviewed his forces, which were in a spirited condition. He found they consisted of 120,000 horse, 2,000 chariots armed with scythes, and 600,000 foot.

When Cyrus judged he had sufficiently regulated his affairs at Babylon, he thought proper to take a journey into Persia. On his way thither he went through Media, to visit Darius, to whom he carried many presents, telling him at the same time that he would find a noble palace at Babylon ready prepared for him whenever he should please to go thither. After a brief stay in Persia, he returned to Babylon, accompanied by his uncle, where they counseled together a scheme of government for the whole empire.

The fame of Daniel, as one who had served under so many kings in Babylon, and also as one to whom the gods had imparted a miraculous degree of wisdom, was spread throughout the city and provinces of Babylon; and, since his appearance before the king as the interpreter of the mysterious handwriting on the night of the fatal banquet, his name was held in great reverence by all the dignitaries of that city.

In a magnificent apartment of the king's palace in the conquered city of Babylon, sat together, in earnest conversation, Darius the Mede, and Cyrus the hero of Persia.

"Thou well sayest that he is neither a Mede nor a Persian," said Cyrus, "neither is he a Chaldean. He was brought from the land of Judah, a captive, about the commencement of Nebuchadnezzar's reign. From what I can learn of his history, he was soon placed under tutors, and outstripped all his companions and became a great favorite of the, king. He was soon elevated to posts of honor, and, with the exception of short intervals, he has been the first officer in the kingdom for more than threescore years. He receives wonderful revelations from the gods, and the fall of Babylon came to pass according to his predictions. Now, uncle, to me it appears far more important to secure the services of an individual, be he even a foreigner, whose head is filled with wisdom and his heart with charity, than to place far inferior personages to fill important offices because they are Medes or Persians. We have many wise men among us, but among this people, whose manners and customs are so different from our own, I fear we have none that can rule with that profound wisdom which has always marked the course of this Hebrew sage. I consider him by far the safest man to appoint as the chief president."

"In this most surely the illustrious son of my brother shall be gratified," replied the Mede. "But why may we not have a short interview with this wonderful man, who appears to have more the attributes of a god than a mortal? Wouldst thou not be pleased to see him?"

"Well pleased."

"Then I shall send for him without delay."

A messenger was, therefore, hurried to the house of the ex-Prime Minister of the Babylonian empire.

The Hebrew soon made his appearance, and such was the calm dignity of his bearing, as he slowly walked into the presence of his superiors, that both the Mede and the Persian unconsciously found themselves on their feet to receive him.

"Our distinguished friend has readily complied with our request," said the Persian, beckoning Daniel to a seat on his right.

"Throughout the days of my pilgrimage it has been my great pleasure to render strict obedience to the will of my superiors in all things consistent with the law of my God."

"Then thou considerest the law of thy God as having stronger claims on thy obedience than the laws of thy king?"

"The law of Jehovah is supreme! By that law my life has been shaped; and now, at its close, it is surely my joy and consolation."

"Precious sentiments from a noble Hebrew!" cried Cyrus, with feeling. "And how long hast thou been a resident of Babylon?"

"Threescore and six years have passed away since thy servant bade adieu to his native hills in the land of Judah, and came to this great city of Babylon. The companions of my early days have mostly passed away, and soon thy servant shall follow them."

"I trust that such a life shall be precious in the sight of the gods for many years to come. Such is thy deep experience in the affairs of state, that we have purposed in our hearts to appoint thee first president of the provinces. Is Belteshazzar willing to serve the king in this capacity, and shed honor upon the joint reign of the Medes and Persians?"

"My life, for the short period I may tarry among mortals, if ye consider me worthy, will be consecrated to your service."

"Then, O Belteshazzar," answered Darius, "thou art, by our united power and authority, appointed chief of the presidents. May the gods be thy support!"

Soon after his appointment, Daniel, in humble reverence, left the presence of the royal dignitaries, and slowly directed his footsteps towards his own mansion.

"The praises of this man have not yet reached his real merits, Cyrus," said Darius. "Thou well sayest. There is a striking peculiarity in all his movements that convinces the beholder that he is one among ten thousand."

"Thy stay in Babylon must be of short duration. Thou art soon off to the wars. I also must soon return to Media; therefore, this appointing of the presidents must be attended to without delay. On thee, I pray, let this business rest; and whomsoever, in thy wisdom, thou shalt appoint, be assured the appointment will receive my cordial approbation."

"In this I will strive to do the will of my kind uncle. I will call together my council, and the thing shall soon be accomplished."

· · · · · ··

In the mansion of one of the presidents, in a delightful part of the city of Babylon, sat together two men in deep and earnest conversation. One of these, whose name was Kinggron, was the owner of the superb mansion. The other, whose name was Fraggood, was his fellow president, under Daniel. On some point of great moment they appeared to be well agreed; while envy, mingled with anger, rested on each countenance.

"The king will soon be again in Babylon," said Kinggron, "and there is no time to be lost. Whatever measure we resort to in order to replace this old Hebrew, whose eye is upon us continually, must be attended to without delay, for the king's stay among us will be of short duration."

"As soon as our companions come, I trust we shall be able to contrive some measure that will remove this ever-watchful old Israelite far out of our way. Does it not ill become the wisdom of Cyrus the Persian to place over our heads this exacting old stranger, who is neither a Persian, Mede, nor even a Chaldean, but a Hebrew, brought to the country as a captive of war - and behold, surely he stands next to the king! One year has gone. We have borne our grief in painful silence.

The time for action has arrived - he must be removed. Our combined wisdom must be brought to bear on this one point, and no rest must we find until it is fully accomplished."

The door opened and four persons silently walked into the apartment. They were of middle age, and appeared to be on familiar terms with the two presidents. They were all Medes, and appeared to be princes of the provinces, and it was very soon evident that with the two superior officers they were favorites.

"Let it be well understood," said Kinggron, "that this Daniel is greatly in the favor of Cyrus; and, moreover, that he stands high in the estimation of the king. Of Cyrus we have no present fear, seeing he is out in the wars. This is well, for before him we would not dare to complain. The king is in possession of far less power of discernment than he, and with him, I trust, we must be successful."

"But," answered Bimbokrak, "we must have some cause - something specific to offer as a ground of complaint against him before the king, or the movement will utterly fail, and prove disastrous to ourselves."

"Thou art right, my good friend," answered the president, "perfectly right. There must be a ground of complaint, and I trust we shall be able to find it. We must find it!"

# CHAPTER XXV.

AGAIN the great city of Babylon was all excitement, and expectation was raised to its highest pitch. The long-expected day had arrived, and the grand entry of Darius the Mede was momentarily expected by an enthusiastic and curious throng. By the Babylonians generally, their new king was regarded in a favorable light. Such had been the profligacy and tyranny of their late kings, that any change was hailed with gratitude; and, moreover, the mildness of Darius toward them on a previous visitation, when accompanied by Cyrus the Persian, had won their regard and affection. Thousands of the people had gone without the walls to meet him, and tens of thousands were seen thronging the public grounds in the vicinity of the royal palaces. At last the monarch's triumphal train appeared in the distance, the shining spears and bright armor of his guard glittering in the clear sunbeams. Nearer and nearer they approached, and entered the city; and, amid enthusiastic shouts, the monarch was escorted to the royal palace.

Darius the Mede was far from being a man of stern moral worth and true decision of character. He was rather weak in mind and easily flattered. Nevertheless he was a man of tender feelings, and cruelty was no part of his nature. He was greatly elated with the warm reception he had received at the hands of the Babylonians, and now or never was the time for the foul conspirators to try their power with the king.

The two presidents, accompanied by the four princes, soon made their appearance in the presence of the king.

"Welcome into the presence of your sovereign!" said the king in a pleasant mood. "Let the full desires of your hearts be made known to the king, and with pleasure he will grant your every wish."

"O king, live forever!" replied President Fraggood. "Thou art a mighty ruler. Thy dominions are unbounded. Thy rich possessions are found in every clime. The name of Darius falls on the ears of the kings of the earth, and they tremble. In thy wisdom thou hast set over the provinces of Babylon an hundred and twenty princes, and over these thou hast set three presidents, the first of whom is Daniel, a man mighty in wisdom and understanding. Now, O king, thou knowest that these provinces are united, and may the gods forbid that anything should ever transpire to dissolve this glorious union. Thy servants have some reason to fear that among some of the inhabitants of these northern provinces there is a disposition to think that the commands of the king are not absolute, and that in certain cases they may be disregarded. Far be it from us to think that this feeling prevails to any serious extent. We are happy to know that, in all the southern provinces, they are abundantly loyal; and, indeed, in the northern provinces this rebellious and dangerous disposition is confined to a few mischievous fanatics; but it is a poisonous plant, O king, that must be destroyed in the bud. If such looseness is permitted to go unpunished, how long will it be before our beloved union is shivered to ruined fragments? We have had this subject under our most serious consideration. We have thought over it with throbbing hearts. Some measure must be resorted to that will impress the inhabitants with the matchless greatness of our king, and convince them that, when he commands, he intends to be obeyed. Therefore, O king, with nothing but the good of the nation at heart, thy servants the three presidents, with all the princes, have enacted this law, and it is now presented to thee for thy royal signature and seal:

"'It is hereby enacted, for the safety of the Union: Let no person offer any prayer or petition to any god or man, except the king, for the space of thirty days; and whosoever shall violate this decree shall be taken and thrown into the den of lions.

"'Given under my hand, at the city of Babylon, on this twelfth day of the ninth month, and sealed with the seal of the Medes and Persians, which changeth not.'"

"In this, surely, there is nothing unreasonable," said the easily flattered king. "My wise presidents and faithful princes could never propose and advocate a measure that was not highly beneficial in its results. That which has any tendency to weaken the glorious bond of our union must be put down, and the safety of the united provinces must be placed on an immovable basis. If, in your superior wisdom, ye have judged that this law is called for, may the gods forbid that I should refuse to give it countenance."

"The measure shall be hailed with universal joy, O king, among all thy loyal subjects, and let those who dare disobey suffer the consequence! From this day the name of Darius the Mede shall be a terror to every evil doer, and all his enemies shall be put to shame."

"Let the king have the writing."

The writing was delivered over to the monarch by a hand that trembled with excitement.

"It is surely a peculiar enactment," said the king, as he took the pen in his hand. "I fail to see its strong points, but at this stage of my reign I am not prepared to oppose a measure that is the offspring of the combined wisdom of the realm. If my Persian nephew were present, I would deem it advisable to have his opinion; but, as he is out in the wars, I cannot avail myself of that."

So the king's name was given to the fatal parchment; and, moreover, it was sealed with the seal of the Medes and Persians.

"The thing is done," said Darius. "Is there anything more that ye wish to communicate to the king?"

"Thy goodness is ever abundant, O king," answered Fraggood. "This is all that we have to present this day. Will the king accept our united gratitude for the kind manner in which we have been received into the presence of the mightiest monarch that ever swayed a scepter? Long live our matchless king! We shall no longer trespass on thy time. We return to our respective stations, to carry out the pleasure of our king."

The conspirators, with bounding hearts, made their way in haste and entered the house of President Fraggood, and there gave vent to the fiendish joy of their malicious hearts at the success of their nefarious scheme.

"Now we must be on the watch," said Kinggron, "or he will, after all, escape. Let three of our number be appointed, and let them be called 'The Union Safety Committee,' whose business it shall be to mark well the movements of the old Hebrew, and prepare, for all emergencies, ready answers for the ears of the king."

"Thou hast well thought," answered Fraggood, "for I apprehend that as yet we are not quite out of danger. I fear this measure will be repulsive to the king, when he thinketh of it in all its parts; and more repulsive still, when he finds the first transgressor to be none other than the first president. Let us be prepared for the mighty contest! This is a movement that will justify desperate measures. Things must be resorted to that, in other matters, would be justly condemned. The object in view must justify our every step. Our words have gone forth to the king that this law is the fruit of the calm deliberations of all the presidents. Now, in regard to the future of this matter, there must be no cowardly apologies, no lame explanations, no faltering embarrassment, nor weak equivocation. Let us still unitedly adhere to every statement that we have made. And shall the testimony of one be strong enough to impeach the testimony of six men? Nay, verily! Let us, therefore, be firm, and we shall not only succeed in condemning the old Israelite, but also prove him a liar. Are we now ready to swear solemnly, in the presence of the gods, that our testimonies, if called before the king, shall say that this Daniel was concerned in framing this law?"

" All ready , most noble Fraggood!" was the

united reply.

"Then we swear!"

The next day, by order of the presidents, the streets of Babylon rang with the proclamation of the new law. Heralds were sent to and fro, who, at the top of their voices, sounded the peculiar edict throughout every thoroughfare. At first it was thought by many to be a mischievous hoax, but it was soon found to be stern reality. Nothing could exceed the astonishment and consternation produced among the inhabitants when they first heard it; it was so unlike anything they could expect from the mild Mede. Not only among the Hebrews, who were numerous in the city, was this singular law looked upon as monstrous in its nature, but also by the great body of Chaldeans, many of whom were warmly attached to the worship of their gods. The shortness of the period in which it was to be enforced, however, served to quiet them in a manner. Thirty days would soon be over, and then they would closely watch the future movements of their new king.

The "Union Safety Committee" acted well their part. Daniel, perfectly acquainted with all their movements, gave himself no uneasiness. With full confidence in his God, he rolled his burden upon Jehovah, and felt the perfect assurance that all would be well.

To Fraggood and Kinggron the devotional hours of the first president were well known; and at such hour it was necessary that they should, under some pretense, find their way into his worshiping chamber. To find such an excuse was but the work of a moment to those so expert in mischievous plots as the two presidents.

Now when Daniel knew that the writing was signed, when the loud voices of the heralds proclaiming the peculiar enactment fell on his ears, he laid by his parchment, closed his eyes for a moment in silent devotion, then rose and calmly entered that little chamber, where he had so often, for so many years, bowed before the God of his fathers. There he had sat for many hours in silent meditation on the length of Judah's captivity, and cried, "How long, O Lord, how long!" A dear spot to the man of God that little chamber had been for many a long year.

"From the days of my childhood I have prayed to the God of my fathers," soliloquized Daniel. "I well remember when, by the side of my mother, while I was yet but a little child, I bowed the knee in humble adoration of my God. From that day to this, throughout my long, weary pilgrimage, I have always prayed and offered my petitions to the Most High. And am I now to be frightened in my old age from the worship of my God through the fear of the lions? Is this the strength of Daniel's faith? I laugh to scorn their blasphemous law!"

Soon after Daniel had left for his devotional exercises, the members of the "Union Safety Committee" (Fraggood, Bimbokrak and Scramgee) were seen on their way from the house of Kinggron, moving in the direction of the house of the first president.

"If we find him in prayer before his God," said Fraggood, "we shall not be called upon to offer any excuse for our calling. We will ask forgiveness for the intrusion and retire. But if we find him otherwise, our object seems reasonable indeed."

"May the gods grant that we need not speak of our object," said Bimbokrak.

By this time the "committee" had arrived at the door of the mansion. Fraggood led the way into the office; but the first president was not there.

"Hark ye!" whispered Fraggood. "Hark!"

"It is the voice of prayer!" said Bimbokrak.

"Silently! Silently!" answered Scramgee, "or he will surely hear us."

"Follow me!" said the president. "Tread lightly!"

The "committee," with beating hearts and light footsteps, sought the chamber whence came the sound of prayer. They soon found the spot; the door was open, and the man of God, on his bended knees, was engaged in solemn devotion.

They gazed upon him for a moment; he saw them not, for his countenance was turned in another direction. Fraggood did not wish to return without acquainting Daniel of his presence, but still he wished to escape an interview. Therefore, in a voice that the first president would surely hear, he said:

"We beg pardon for this intrusion. Let us not disturb our most excellent friend whilst he makes his petitions to his God."

The Hebrew prophet gently turned his head, but he saw only the receding forms of the members of the "committee" as they hastened to the street below, and so he continued his supplications to the God of his fathers.

The "Union Safety" men were soon back again at the house of President Kinggron, and great was the demonstration of joy at the promised success of their malignant plot.

The next morning witnessed again the guilty form of the leading conspirator, with his two accomplices, on the way towards the king's palace. They were admitted, and were soon in the presence of their king.

"And what good thing do the presidents desire of the king?" asked Darius, in rather a surly mood, for, the more he thought of their new statute, the more repulsive it appeared in his sight.

"O king, live forever!" replied Fraggood, with a deceitful smile on his countenance. "Hast thou not signed a decree that every man that asketh a petition of any god or man for thirty days, save of thee, O king, shall be cast into the den of lions?"

"The thing is true," answered the king, "according to the laws of the Medes and Persians, which altereth not."

"Then it is made our painful duty to inform thee that Daniel, which is of the children of the captivity of Judah, regardeth not thee, O king, nor the decree that thou has signed; but maketh his petition three times a day."

"Daniel!" replied the king. "I know of no Daniel but my worthy first president, whom ye say assisted in making this law."

"This same Daniel, O king, thy first president, is the guilty one!" answered Fraggood. "After having exerted his influence with thy servants to make the law, he is now the first of all to transgress. In this he hath but sought an opportunity to show thee, O king, how utterly he disregardeth all thy wise commandments."

"What!" said the king, suddenly rising to his feet. "Daniel, the first president in the kingdom? Daniel, noted for his wisdom and prudence? Impossible! Ye have been wrongly informed! Beware how ye thus accuse the best man in Babylon!"

"Thy servants wonder not at thy astonishment, O king! If we had not been eye-witnesses to the thing, we could have in no wise believed it; but the eyes and ears of thy servants are witnesses against him. He offers his petitions, and tramples upon the authority of our king."

"His petitions!" cried the excited king. "And to whom does he offer his petitions?"

"He daily offers his petitions to his God, O king!"

"His God! Wiseman! Who can - But - If - Say ye not that Daniel was concerned in making this law?"

"Yea, verily, O king! May the gods forbid that we should utter aught but truth in the presence of King Darius!"

"To me it seemeth a strange thing that Daniel, the worshiper of the God of Israel, should frame a law that bears oppressively on himself and upon thousands of his nation within the realm. And it seemeth still more strange to the king that he should be the first transgressor! Already have I sorrow of heart because I signed the decree; but the thing is done, and my name must go down to posterity as the name of a fool. There is a mystery connected with this affair that to me, as yet, is inexplicable. If by any means I find that I have been wrongly dealt with, by all the gods I swear I will pour vengeance on the guilty heads!"

"If thou wilt permit the four princes to testify, they will say, with thy servant, that this Daniel was the chief mover in the formation of this law."

"At present I have no desire to hear from any of the princes. But to think of casting Daniel into the den of lions is mournful beyond description - it must not be done!"

"So say we all, O king, when we consult our feelings; but the decree is signed according to the law of the Medes and Persians, and cannot be altered. The honor of the king depends upon the faithful execution of all his laws; and if in this one point thou failest and let the guilty one escape, thy subjects will laugh at thy timidity, and lawlessness will prevail throughout our borders."

"Of this we may speak hereafter. I must see the first president and learn more of this matter ere I take another step in this unhappy affair."

On the departure of the conspirators, the king immediately sent for Daniel, and soon the Hebrew prophet stood in the presence of Darius the Mede. On his countenance rested that same calm smile. The king gazed upon him for a moment, and could not but notice the contrast between the serene, noble countenance of the Hebrew prophet, and the uneasy, agitated visage of President Fraggood.

"Thou standest before the king, O Daniel, accused as an evil doer! What sayest thou for thyself?"

"What is the nature of thy servant's offense, O king?"

"Thou art accused of violating a law, chiefly of thine own making, by offering thy petitions to thy God. To the king it seemeth strange indeed that he who was the first mover in the formation of a new law, should be the first one to transgress it. What meaneth all this?"

"I readily perceive by the words of thy mouth, O king, that thou hast been greatly deceived in this matter. Thy servant had nothing to do in forming a law whose every feature is repulsive to his soul and an insult to the God he worshipeth. This law came from the enemies of thy servant, for the purpose of his overthrow. Having failed in every other point, with malicious hearts they have brought forward this measure, knowing well that I could never yield it my obedience. With lying tongues have they declared before thee that it received my approbation. It is true, O king, that I have violated thy law; and, moreover, I must do so hereafter. For fourscore years has thy servant offered his prayers to the God of his fathers. When a little lad in the land of Judah, I was taught by a beloved mother to lisp the name of Jehovah. From that time to this, O king, at morning, noon and eventide, thy servant has prayed to his God. And is Daniel to be frightened from his duty now in his old age? Nay, O king! My prayers must daily ascend to the throne of the Most High! Sooner would I suffer a thousand deaths than prove a traitor to the God of Israel."

The king was deeply moved by the words of the aged Hebrew, and continued for some time in deep silence. At last he rose to his feet, and, with a voice trembling with anger, exclaimed:

"By the gods! If these presidents have come before me with lying words, I will cut them in pieces, and leave them neither root nor branch! Daniel, if thou sayest, I will have them arrested and destroyed! This very hour the word shall go forth!"

"Nay, O king! Listen to the counsel of thine aged servant. This hasty movement would not be well received among thy subjects. The decree has gone forth. I pray thee let the law have its course, but be assured, O king, that not a hair of thy servant's head shall be injured. The God that I serve and in whom I trust, shall deliver me from every danger, and no weapon formed against me shall prosper. Hereafter do with mine enemies as thou seest fit. Be assured, O king, that my life is as secure among the lions as in the presence of my kind sovereign! The same God that preserved my cousins alive in the midst of a burning, fiery furnace, can easily shut the mouths of the lions, and make them as harmless as the little lambs of the flock."

Here the king was melted into tears; and, so deeply was he affected, that for a long time he was unable to speak. At last, in a low key, he spoke:

"O Daniel, this thing must never come to pass! May the gods forbid that I should endanger the life of my servant! But the writing is signed! My heart is sad! My soul is sick!"

"Let not the king be sore troubled on account of his servant," said Daniel. "The God of heaven shall certainly overrule this matter to his own glory."

"Thou mayest return, Daniel," said the king. "I know not what to do. I fear I have been greatly deceived."

"The word of thy servant, in a case like this, is not sufficient to gainsay the testimony of six witnesses. When the proper hour arrives, the king shall learn from other lips than mine the deep iniquity of these foul conspirators. Adieu, O king! Let Jehovah use his own measures for the vindication of his own law!" And the first president left the royal presence.

On that night Darius the Mede laid his head on his pillow with the full purpose of delivering Daniel.

Early on the morrow, the "Union Safety Committee," accompanied by the other three, made their way into the presence of the king.

"Ye are punctual!" said the king, with a meaning glance.

"We take unbounded pleasure in obeying all the requirements of our king," said Fraggood, "and may the gods curse all those that are disobedient!"

"Since ye left my presence yesterday, I have had an interview with the first president, and from his venerable lips I learn that he had no voice in the formation of this law that ye say he hath violated."

"This is as thy servant expected, O king!" answered Kinggron. "What transgressor do we ever find that will not strive to hide his guilt?"

"Daniel strives not to hide his guilt," replied the king in a firm tone. "He freely acknowledges that he violated the law, and moreover he assures me that he will continue to violate it three times every day. Thus ye perceive that the first president wishes not to hide his guilt, nor even to escape the punishment. But with all the weight of reason, consistency and humanity on his side, he pronounces the law at war with all goodness, and denies having had any part in bringing it into existence. Now, with all due respect to your testimonies, which, in point of law, must outweigh the declaration of one man, I freely acknowledge to you, my presidents and princes, that it is my firm conviction that ye are a band of unprincipled liars, fully bent on the destruction of this Daniel!"

At this plain, royal truth, the "Union Safety Committee" turned pale, and the other three appeared to be similarly affected. But Fraggood, recovering his self-possession, hastened to the rescue.

"Then my lord the king had rather believe a man that defies his power by boasting his determination to violate the king's decree at least three times a day, than his faithful servants who honor his laws, and who desire to bring the guilty to punishment. Let not the king be deceived by the smooth tongue of this intriguing old Israelite, who can by the eloquence of his lips give to truth the color of falsehood, and to deception the appearance of sincerity. Thy servants now in the presence of the king are ready to prove all the declarations of thy servants who testified in thy presence yesterday. But what would avail their testimony in the ears of Darius? But, O king, remember that thy decree hath gone forth, and it cannot be recalled. And, moreover, it is well understood in Babylon that Daniel sets thy power at defiance, and thy decision in this matter is watched for by tens of thousands; and if this Daniel escapes the punishment of the law, we may as well burn up our statute books and give absolute liberty to every ruffian and desperado. Law and order will be at an end, the union of the provinces will be forever dissolved, and confusion and desolation shall follow. The question now to be settled is not, 'How came this law to be enacted?' but, seeing that it is enacted, is there power enough in the king of the Medes and Persians to put it in force; and, if there is, will he do it? Or does he wish us to retire from his presence and send forth heralds through the streets of Babylon to inform the people that the decree enacted a few days ago, and signed according to the law of the Medes and Persians, which changeth not, is abolished? Shall it be told in the streets of this proud city that Darius the Mede has so quickly changed his mind and is sorry for what he hath done, because one of his favorites has violated the law? Thou saidst yesterday that thy name would go down to posterity as the name of a fool. The king was far from being believed by thy servant then, but, if thou persistest in this determination of letting the guilty escape, I know not but thou wilt cause to be brought about the fulfillment of thine own prophecy?"

Long and severe was this interview between the king and the conspirators, and all the weight of their ingenuity was brought to bear on his mind. It failed to convince him that Daniel's words were false; yet, partly from a false view of consistency, and partly from the advice of the first president, he gave his signature to the death warrant of the old Israelite.

# CHAPTER XXVI.

THE news of the condemnation of the Hebrew prophet soon spread through all Babylon, and the hour of his execution was well known. It was the great theme of conversation among high and low, rich and poor, and there were but few who were not horrified at the awful doom of the man of God.

No man in Babylon was better known or more universally beloved than the old prime minister of Nebuchadnezzar. His long residence in the city had rendered his name familiar to the populace, and a vast number held him in respect bordering on veneration. His mild and friendly deportment whenever brought into the society of the common people, had won their affection. The poor and the needy had ever found relief at his door. The little children even claimed the aged prophet as their friend. He found it not beneath the dignity of his station to speak to them in the street, put his hand on their heads, and say, "May Jehovah bless my little children!"

In the vicinity of the first president's mansion were seen numerous groups of persons engaged in low conversation, while deep sorrow was visible on every countenance. These gatherings gradually swelled to one solid mass of human beings. The doors of the president's house were closed, and thick curtains' were drawn across the lattices, and no one as yet appeared to enter those portals. Presently the throng was in commotion, several chariots halted before the door, and a number of government officials alighted, and, with slow steps, and solemn countenances, they ascended the steps, entered, and closed the door. A peculiar gathering that! A solemn, sad throng! All conversation had ceased. The stillness was broken by the sudden appearance of several platoons of soldiers, who took their stand and formed a square in front of the mansion. The door at last opened, and two uniformed officers appeared side by side, and slowly marched out. Next appeared the sheriff, with the prisoner leaning on his arm. On the broad platform he waited for a moment, evidently to permit some of his near friends to embrace him before they parted. Thick and fast they gathered around the aged saint, with loud weeping and lamentation; but soon their cries were drowned amid the louder lamentations of the throng. Last of all there approached the man of God two aged women, on whose countenances Time had tried in vain to erase marks of loveliness and beauty.

With a smile, one of the twain took the hand of the prophet, and gently said:

"May Jehovah grant a happy night to his servant among the lions, and on the morrow may we have a joyful meeting."

"God bless thee, dear Perreeza!" said the man of God.

The other one now approached, and, in a mild voice, said:

"Daniel, the servant of the living God, is secure in the

midst of all his foes. He that quenched the violence of the fire, shall tame the fury of the lions."

"Heaven smile upon the daughter of Barzello!" was the prophet's answer.

The procession was now formed, and soon reached the vicinity of the lions' den, where thousands of the inhabitants had assembled to take the last lingering look at their aged fellow-citizen. There also was the king himself, with a number of his most intimate nobles. The soldiers moved forward, and a clear space was prepared in front of the platform on which the king and his friends stood.

The countenance of the monarch was pale, and his whole appearance gave the beholder to understand that he was one of the unhappiest of mortals. The conspirators were not permitted to occupy the platform with him, but were commanded to stand together on his left.

When the prisoner arrived, he gently bowed and saluted the king, which salutation was answered only by falling tears. The throng, witnessing the emotion of the king, gave vent to their grief, and one loud wail ascended. Then, indeed, did those conspirators tremble! Then did they really learn the deep hold their victim had on the popular mind. Again the agitation was partially quieted, when the loud roaring of lions within made the earth tremble. The awful moment was drawing nigh! Daniel ascended some steps near by, and having had permission from the king, proceeded, in a few words, to address the multitude:

"Babylonians! with naught of malice in my heart against any man, and with perfect good feeling toward the king, I yield myself to the demands of a broken law. Here, in the presence of the God of my fathers, whom I worship, and in the presence of my king, whom I respect, and in the presence of this throng, whose tears flow for my sorrow, and in the presence of these mine accusers, who thirst for my blood, I solemnly declare, that as first president in the kingdom, I never was consulted in regard to the making of this law, that is about to consign your aged servant to the lions. In honor to my king, who now laments the sad fate of his unworthy president, let me also testify that in order to persuade him to sign a decree which had never entered his heart, the most deliberate falsehoods were poured into his ears, by those whose only object was the overthrow of Daniel. After more than threescore years of public service, I cheerfully submit to my fate, knowing well that Jehovah, the God of Israel, in whom I trust, will direct this whole matter to his own glory. Hereafter it will be known in Babylon, that it was not the 'safety of the Union' that demanded the enactment of this cruel law; but that it was conceived in envy, and brought forth in malice, and thoughtlessly signed by our king, who considered all his presidents to be men of benevolence, wisdom, and understanding. For violating this law I ask no forgiveness. Sooner would I suffer a thousand deaths than prove a traitor to the religion of my fathers. Babylonians, I say no more! Accept my thanks for your tears! May Jehovah continue to grant you great prosperity, when your friend Daniel shall have passed away."

Then turning to those whose painful duty it was to lead him to the den, he said:

"Now I am ready."

The executioners, with trembling hands, laid hold of the aged prisoner, and led him to the door of the den. Again there was an awful roaring of lions. As he passed the king on his way to the den, the monarch cried out:

"Thy God, whom thou servest continually, he will surely deliver thee!"

The prisoner was seized with strong hands and elevated over the inner walls, and by means of strong cords was lowered to the bottom of the den, where the ravenous lions held their nightly revels. The executioners, as if afraid to hear the prisoner's dying shrieks, hastened away. The throng soon dispersed in sorrowful silence. The king, in deep agony of mind, entered his chariot, and was driven to the palace.

How sad was that night for royalty! Filled with remorse for having signed the fatal decree, and knowing not how to retrace his steps or to retrieve the effects of his rash act, the king passed the hours in agony. With a heavy heart and a throbbing brow, he paced the length of his royal bedchamber, and thus did he converse with himself:

"How he justified the king, almost with his dying breath! Ah! but I justify not myself. Why did I sign that silly and cruel decree, by which the prime jewel of my kingdom is lost? Why did I not consider the thing well, and consult the first president? Alas! it is now too late. The deed is done, and there is no remedy! How the multitude sympathized with the noble prisoner! How copious their tears and how audible their sobs! How beloved in the estimation of the populace was that aged Daniel! What think they by this time of my prudence and wisdom? Have I not lost in this the estimation of my people? Will his God, indeed, deliver him? Is he not already torn by the lions? How cruel a fate for so worthy a man! But if Daniel is spared, no thanks to me! Will not this people inwardly curse me, and wish me out of their borders? What poor returns to them, for the grand reception they gave me! What will my nephew, Cyrus, think of my sagacity and power of discernment!"

· · · · · ··

Let us for a while leave the unfortunate Mede, and take a view of the hero of the lions' den.

When Daniel was thrust among the lions, the sun was yet one hour above the western horizon, and the light from the top of the den, made the interior comparatively light. When he found himself at the bottom, for a minute he walked to and fro, then fell on his knees, and began to pour his prayers into the ears of the God of his fathers. The lions, quite unaccustomed to such a sight, looked on for a while in silent wonder. Then they ran together to the other end of the den, where the old lion of all - the "lord of the manor" - and his aged companion, the old lioness, the mistress of the "establishment," were, heedless of the youthful pranks and occasional quarrels of their offspring, enjoying a good, comfortable sleep. A loud roar from one of the youngsters, which was answered by another louder roar from his companion, aroused the energies of the old couple. They uttered an ill-natured growl, very much on the same principle that anyone else would on being unnecessarily disturbed in the midst of a nap. Perhaps the growl was equivalent to, "Children, you are very rude. Make less noise, or I shall attend to you!" This reproof (if reproof it was) did not seem in the least to frighten the young lions. One of them, the one that roared the loudest, put his head close to that of his sire, and if he said anything, it was in so low a whisper that it could not be heard at any distance. From what immediately followed, one might think the young chap said something in this fashion:

"Get up quickly! Come to the other end of the den, and there you will see a sight that you never saw before in all your days. There is another victim; but he has no more the appearance of common victims than thou hast. I know by his eye he has no fear of the lions. Why, think! as soon as he came to the bottom of the den, he walked to and fro among us as deliberately as my brother here, or myself, would walk among our companions."

After the whispering was over (if whispering it was), the old lion uttered another growl, as much as to say, "That sounds to me rather improbable, but I guess I will go and see for myself." The old lion led the way. Close by his heels followed the lioness. Next in order followed the rest of the family. They soon arrived at the spot, and sure enough, it was as the young lion had declared. The old lion paused for a moment, but he soon made up his mind that there was nothing to fear. So he slowly approached. He paused again. Daniel reached out his hand and spoke. The lion fancied the peculiarity of that voice; so with eyes half closed he slowly walked up to the man, and with the innocence and harmlessness of a young spaniel, he licked the hand of the prophet. After having partially conquered his embarrassment, he uttered another low growl, and looked toward the rest of the company, as much as to say, "Come this way! Don't be afraid."

They slowly and silently gathered around the strange visitor, and each one appeared to be pleased to be permitted to come in contact with his person in some way. And when the darkness of night gathered around them, the old lion answered for Daniel's pillow, the lioness lay at his feet, and the young lions stretched themselves on either side, to keep him warm; and soon the Prophet of Jehovah was fast asleep.

· · · · · · ·

If ever a sleepless mortal, wearied with the tediousness of a painful night, rejoiced to see the first glimmering dawn of the morn, King Darius did, after that dark, dreary period of agony. No sooner was it fairly day than the monarch ordered his chariot, and, with a number of his nobles, he was once more on his way toward the den of lions. The royal chariot, as it moved through the various thoroughfares, attracted the notice of the inhabitants. Its destination was understood, and as there was some faint hope in the minds of thousands that the God of Daniel would miraculously interfere and save his servant, they had accordingly held themselves in readiness to be early at the den. They, therefore, with all haste followed in the direction of the royal train. The king was greatly astonished to find already there a large number of the inhabitants. The movements and excitement of the people had also brought to the spot the six conspirators, who were greatly astonished to see the king. The monarch, in trembling accents, ordered the stone to be removed from the door of the den. The order was quickly obeyed. While every eye rested upon him, the king entered and stood inside of the outer door, and cried, in a loud voice:

"Oh, Daniel! is thy God, whom thou servest continually, able to deliver thee from the lions?"

Oh, the breathless silence of that moment! A thousand hearts throb with deep emotion, in painful suspense to learn the result. Hark! A voice clear and firm ascends from the depths, and falls on the ears of the multitude:

"O king, live forever!"

It was enough! Gladsome shouts echoed from a thousand tongues! The joy was unbounded. Their sorrow for their old friend was turned into joy, and the name of the God of Daniel was praised.

Immediate orders were given to bring the old Hebrew up, and soon he stood in the presence of the king and the rejoicing throng.

Then said Daniel, turning to the king, "My God hath sent his angel, and hath shut the mouths of the lions, that they have not hurt me; forasmuch as before him innocency was found in me; and also before thee, O king, have I done no hurt."

An aged man at this moment was seen making his way through the crowd, as if endeavoring to find admittance into the presence of the king. His venerable appearance served to make for him room.

"We meet again, Apgomer!" cried Daniel, in a familiar, friendly voice: and then to the king he said:

"This is my good friend Apgomer, O king, one of the few friends of my early days. He hath words to communicate to the king, in the presence of this throng, that will give thee to understand clearly that this law was prepared on purpose to ensnare thy servant Daniel."

"Let my worthy friends, Fraggood and Kinggron, with their four companions, the princes, stand in this direction!" said the king, with an angry expression of countenance.

The conspirators, with paleness gathering on their brows, obeyed, and tremblingly stood facing the king.

"Now, O Daniel, thy friend Apgomer may give his testimony before the king."

"O king, live forever!" said Apgomer. "This day thy servant is fourscore and ten years old. From the days of my childhood have I dwelt in Babylon; and never for any long period have I departed hence. Soon thy servant shall leave this world of sorrow - I stand on the verge of the grave. At this time, with deep soberness, I appeal to the God that dwelleth in light for the sincerity of my purpose in thus appearing before my lord the king. My words will be few, therefore, O king, I pray thee hear me patiently.

"These men who now stand before thee and by whose continual importunity thou gavest thy signature for the arrest of thy servant Daniel, are wicked and deceitful men, and with lying words have they deceived thee, O king. Their secret devices are well known to thy servant. With mine own ears have I listened to their midnight plotting; and from their own lips have I learned their fixed purpose to destroy the innocent without cause, even thy servant Daniel. For many months, O king, these cruel men have sought an occasion against the first president, and after having failed in every other point, they thought at last of this.

"I heard the plot described at midnight recently while resting in the public garden. The conspiracy was led by Fraggood and Kinggron. They were assisted by a number of the princes, among whom are Bimbokrak and Scramgee. This foul movement has been going on for many a day, but until last week the conspirators could not agree on a plan. At last, Prince Scramgee brought forward a scheme, which met with the cordial approval of the rest. And who but the chief evil spirit of the universe could have put in his heart such a horrible measure? It was in effect that a law be enacted that anyone who prayed to the God of Israel should be cast into the lions' den. When I made thy servant Daniel acquainted with the plot against his life, his only reply was:

"'Let them proceed in their scheme of wickedness. Let it become ripe. The God in whom I trust shall vindicate the honor and superiority of his own law. I might easily frustrate all their malicious designs by acquainting the king with their cowardly plots; but the cause of Jehovah shall gather more strength from a miraculous display of his power in the preservation of his servant from harm. Forty years ago, idolatry in Chaldea received a blow, from the effects of which it has never recovered, in the miraculous deliverance of my three cousins from the midst of a burning, fiery furnace. And if a visit to the lions for a few hours may cause the name of Jehovah to be feared, I ask for no greater honor. No weapon formed against the servant of Jehovah shall prosper. Let not my good friend Apgomer be troubled. The life of Daniel is as safe in the lions' den as among his friends at his own home.

Erasmus W. Jones

Therefore let them proceed with their malicious measures; let no impediment be thrown in their way. Let them have a few days of rejoicing, and their brief nights of merriment. Soon the day of retribution shall overtake them; for He that is higher than the highest shall surely avenge himself on these workers of iniquity.'"

"Believe not this man, O king!" said the pale and trembling Fraggood, "seeing he prepareth lying words before thee."

At this moment a young man, whose countenance denoted some passion, rushed on the stage, and, without any apology or ceremony, began to speak:

"Let not the worthy and aged Apgomer be called a liar! A lie never escaped those venerable lips, O king! As soon may the gods lie! Thy servant is the doorkeeper of the Garden. I can testify to the existence of a plot to destroy Daniel."

"It is enough!" cried the king. "Seize the guilty wretches! Let the cowardly liars meet the doom they had prepared for my servant Daniel! Up! and throw them to the lions!"

No sooner were the words spoken than a score of willing hands seized the forms of the conspirators, and, amid the curses of an indignant throng, they were thrown to the depth of the den, to meet a far different fate from that of the man of God.

Then spoke the king:

"I make a decree, that in every dominion of my

kingdom, men tremble and fear before the God of Daniel: for he is the living God, and steadfast forever, and his kingdom is that which shall not be destroyed, and his dominion shall be even unto the end. He delivereth and rescueth, and he worketh signs and wonders in heaven and on earth, who hath delivered Daniel from the power of the lions."

"O king, live forever!" cried the well pleased throng.

Daniel was taken into the royal chariot and seated by the side of the king, and the royal train moved forward, amid the triumphant shouts of the populace.

Thus fidelity to the God of Israel was abundantly rewarded.

# CHAPTER XXVII.

IN TWO years after these occurrences Darius the Mede died; and about the same time died also Cambyses, the father of Cyrus, in Persia. Cyrus, therefore, returned to Babylon, and took upon himself the government of the empire.

The history of the lions' den, with all the intrigues that led to it, made Daniel thrice dear to the inhabitants of Babylon. His name commanded reverence wherever it was mentioned, He was looked upon as an angel of mercy, goodness, and wisdom, sent by the gods to bless the race.

Cyrus, for a long time, had desired the opportunity of a prolonged interview with Daniel, of whom he had heard so many wonderful things, both as a minister to the king of Babylon and also while administering the affairs of the kingdom under the reign of his Median uncle. The Persian was already well versed in current history. Of the God of Israel he had heard much of late, and he felt a strong inclination to hear more. And of whom could he learn to better advantage than of the famous Hebrew prophet? The celebrated Persian, from his infancy, had been taught to worship and adore the imaginary gods of his own country; but he had always felt doubtful in regard to the existence of these gods; and many of the popular theories of Persia, in regard to their various deities, were, to him, full of inconsistencies and contradictions.

Not many days after his arrival in Babylon, the royal chariot was seen to halt at the door of Daniel's residence; and, moreover, the king himself was seen to enter.

"Thou wilt pardon this sudden intrusion," said Cyrus; "I have long desired an interview with the president, and for this purpose I have entered his house; the king is happy to find that he is not absent."

"My lord the king hath greatly honored his unworthy servant by entering under his roof," said the old Hebrew. "This condescension of the great Persian conqueror is a favor of such a magnitude that it shall never be forgotten."

"Let not my aged friend Daniel speak thus," said the king, in a friendly manner. "Call it not condescension in Cyrus to seek the society of one who has justly earned the reputation of being the most profound statesman that ever moved among mortals. Let the king rather consider himself honored in being permitted to listen to thy words of wisdom and understanding."

"Humility becometh well the potentates of earth. But yet, O king, thou beholdest not the real grandeur of thy mission. Thou knowest not that thou art the peculiarly anointed - not of the gods, but of the only God of heaven, the Almighty Jehovah, the God of Israel, to pour his wrath upon the nations, and to restore the children of Judah to their own land."

"Thou hast touched a theme on which , above all

others, at this time, the king would choose to dwell. Of the gods I have but an imperfect knowledge. Conscious am I that under the particular direction of some invisible power I have been led forward in all my movements, from my youth up. I was taught to worship the gods in my juvenile days; but ever since I arrived at years of thought and judgment, my mind has been greatly perplexed by what seemeth to me to be glaring inconsistencies in our theory of religion."

"Praised be the name of Jehovah, under whose direction thou comest at this time to seek knowledge! Happy is thy servant Daniel to know that he is indeed able to impart unto the king that which he inquireth after. Jehovah is the only God, and the signs which he hath in all ages given of himself, O king, are abundant. We hear much of the exploits of the gods of the heathen; but of these performances there are no proofs, and they exist only in the imaginations of their worshipers. Not so with our God - the God that made the world. The history of our nation, which history no one can gainsay, is an assemblage of miracles. Examine the records of our historian Moses, who conversed with God face to face. Our God brought us out from under the dominion of Pharaoh with a strong hand and an outstretched arm. He gave evidence of his presence by the infliction of twelve terrible plagues on the king of Egypt and his people. He opened before the Hebrews a passage through the sea, and brought them dry-shod to the opposite shore. For forty years were they fed with manna from heaven, while water was called forth from the flinty rock. And as the waves of the Red Sea were parted before them as they left Egypt, so, in like manner, were the waters of Jordan parted as they left the plains of Moab; and thus were they settled in the land of Canaan. Since that day, nine hundred and fifteen years have passed away; and during all this period, Jehovah hath given unto his people abundant signs of his presence. Thus our God is not a being that dwells only in the imagination of men, but his wonderful acts, O king, are written on the pages of correct history."

"If these things are so, surely the God of Israel is the only God. But, Daniel, thou knowest that it is much harder for Cyrus the Persian to believe these things than for thee, who art a native Hebrew, and a firm believer in the God thou worshipest. Have not the Persians their histories of their gods as well as ye?"

"They have, O king! But those histories are dark, indefinite, and without date, which is a conclusive evidence that they are fiction, and not history. If my lord the king hath aught to doubt in regard to the correctness of our ancient historians concerning our God, what thinketh he of those miraculous displays of Divine power witnessed by his servant and by thousands more, during the last threescore years and ten?"

"Proceed, Daniel; the king is well pleased to hear thee!"

"Be it known to thee, O king, that all the calamities that of late have befallen Babylon have come to pass in perfect accordance with the predictions of God's prophets, some of whom prophesied over two hundred years before these events transpired. When thou comparest these prophecies with the actual occurrences, there remaineth no longer a place for doubt. Even the draining of the Euphrates, O king, was spoken of by the prophet of Jehovah over one hundred and fifty years before the wonderful thing was conceived in thy mind."

"Enough, O Daniel! Enough!" cried Cyrus. "If thou art able to show me this thing, I ask no more!"

The Hebrew sage, with a peculiar smile of satisfaction on his countenance, rose from his seat, and took from a shelf what appeared to be a scroll of ancient manuscript.

"Listen, O king, to the words of Jehovah's prophets in regard to the taking of Babylon:

"'Make bright the arrows, gather the shields! The Lord hath raised up the spirits of the kings of the Medes, for his device is against Babylon to destroy it; because it is the vengeance of the Lord, the vengeance of his temple. Howl ye, for the day of the Lord is at hand! Shout against her round about! Behold, I will stir up the Modes against them, who shall not regard silver; and as for gold, they shall not delight in it. Lift ye up a banner upon the high mountain! Exalt the voice! shake the hand, that they may go into the gates of the nobles! Go up, O Elam! Besiege, O Media! Therefore shall evil come upon thee, and thou shalt not know from whence it cometh. Desolation shall come upon thee suddenly, which thou shalt not know. I have laid a snare for thee, and thou art also taken, and thou wast not aware. O thou that dwellest upon many waters, I will dry up her sea, and make her springs dry. A drought is upon her waters, and they shall be dried up. In her heat I will make their feasts, and I will make them drunken, that they may repose and sleep a perpetual sleep, and not wake, saith the Lord. Arise, ye princes, and anoint the shield! Prepare slaughter for his children, for the iniquity of their fathers, that they do not rise and possess the land; for I will rise up against thee, saith the Lord of hosts, and cut off from Babylon the name and remnant, and son and nephew, saith the Lord.'

"These, O king, are some of the predictions of Jehovah against Babylon, by the mouths of his holy prophets. And has not my lord the king been an eye witness to their fulfillment!"

"They have all come to pass to the letter, O Daniel! Surely the God of Israel is the God of gods! Why should I any longer doubt? Thus it appears that Cyrus the Persian has been under the directions of the God of Israel, to bring about these wonderful events!"

"In this thou sayest truly, O king. And strange as it may sound in thine ears, be assured that thy name was known in Israel for over one hundred and fifty years before thy birth."

Here the Persian gazed on the Hebrew for awhile in silent wonderment; and it was evident from his countenance, that he had some doubt in regard to the truth of the sentence.

"Did the king rightly understand thy meaning? Sayest thou that my name was known in Israel for one hundred and fifty years previous to my birth?"

"The king rightly understandeth his servant. Thy name was carefully written in a book by one of our prophets two hundred and twenty years ago. Happily, I have now in my possession a copy taken from the original, written by one of our scribes, and bearing date which maketh it over one hundred and seventy years old. If the king desireth, thy servant will read."

"Read, Daniel," said the king, with much feeling.

Daniel from the same scroll from which he had read before, which was the Prophecies of Isaiah, read:

"'Thus saith the Lord to his anointed, to Cyrus, whose right hand I have holden, to subdue nations before him; and I will loose the loins of kings to open before him the two-leaved gates; and the gates shall not he shut, I will go before thee, and make the crooked places straight: I will break in pieces the gates of brass, and cut in sunder the bars of iron: and I will give thee the treasures of darkness, and hidden riches of secret places, that thou mayest know that I, the Lord which call thee by thy name, am the God of Israel. For Jacob my servant's sake, and Israel mine elect, I have even called thee by thy name: I have surnamed thee, though thou hast not known me.'"

The Persian was deeply moved. Indeed, tears were in the monarch's eyes. He rose, and in the deepest reverence, exclaimed:

"I acknowledge the God of Israel as the great ruling power of the universe! Under his infinitely wise directions I stand ready to do his pleasure, and accomplish his great designs."

"One favor it is thine to grant, O king, according to the word of the Lord. For their iniquity the children of Judah were carried captive into Babylon, and Jerusalem was rendered desolate. According to the word of the Lord by the mouth of Jeremiah, they were to remain in this land of their captivity for seventy years. This period, O king, in a few more months will be at an end. I pray thee, give permission to the children of Judah to return to their own land, and build up the old waste places, and raise again a temple to the God of Israel."

"This thy request, O Daniel, shall be granted," said the king, in a firm voice. "The proclamation shall go forth from the king, and all that is needful for the enterprise shall be supplied."

"Praised be Jehovah!" said the aged Hebrew. "At last the days of Judah's captivity are numbered, and Jerusalem shall be restored. Thy God, O king, whom from henceforth thou wilt serve, shall greatly prosper thee in the affairs of thy kingdom."

"I trust my faithful servant will consent to tarry with the king, to whom, from time to time, he will deliver lessons of wisdom. I purpose soon to remove my court from Babylon to Ecbatana, in Persia, whither I hope my faithful servant Daniel will consent to remove."

"Thy servant in this is willing to abide the pleasure of the king."

The king left the presence of his aged minister with strange but yet pleasurable emotions, hurried into his chariot, which was waiting, and was soon on his way to the palace.

The next day the following proclamation was heralded through the streets of Babylon, and sent to all the provinces:

"Thus saith Cyrus, King of Persia: The Lord God of heaven hath given me all the kingdoms of the earth, and he hath charged me to build him an house at Jerusalem, which is in Judah. Who is there among you of all his people? His God be with him, and let him go up to Jerusalem, which is in Judah, and build the house of the Lord God of Israel (he is the God), which is in Jerusalem. And whosoever remaineth in any place where he sojourneth, let the men of his place help him with silver, and with gold, and with goods, and with beasts, besides the free-will offering for the house of God that is in Jerusalem."

This proclamation was received by the captive Jews with gladness and great joy. Measures were immediately put forth for the accomplishment of the enterprise; the king, in the meantime, continuing to give every encouragement to these measures, in the firm conviction that he was under peculiar guidance of the God of heaven.

. . . . . ..

A brighter day never dawned on the plains of Judah. The brilliant rays of the morning sun were seen flashing upwards from behind Mount Zion, like so many messengers in uniform, proclaiming the near approach of their sovereign master. Presently, the great regent of day himself, in slow and silent majesty, made his appearance, and once more smiled on the City of the Great King. At an early hour, multitudes were seen pouring into the city, from east, west, north, and south, and on each countenance might have been read a degree of excitement and animation. This was the twenty-fourth day of the second month, in the second year after the return from Babylon; and on this day was to be laid the foundation of the temple of the Lord. This was well understood throughout the land; and we wonder not that from cities and villages, from hill and valley, the emancipated Hebrews hastened by thousands to witness a scene at the thought of which their hearts throbbed with intense emotions. By the sixth hour the great multitudes had congregated to witness the solemn and joyful ceremony. There stood the priests, with their long, flowing robes, with trumpets in their hands. There, also, stood the Levites, and the sons of Asaph, with cymbals to praise the Lord, after the ordinance of David, king of Israel. The builders had laid the foundation. Then the trumpets were blown, and the sons of Asaph struck their cymbals. Songs of praise ascended on high, and they gave thanks unto the Lord.

The ceremony was over. The concourse was dismissed, under the benediction of the priests, and the masses moved homeward in all directions.

Two chariots of magnificent appearance, drawn by beautiful steeds, were seen leaving the ground. They drew much attention from the crowd, as they leisurely drove through the winding streets of Jerusalem. At last the chariots halted in front of a mansion, which had the appearance of having of late undergone a thorough repair. From one of these chariots alighted several venerable men, their hair whitened with age. Their whole bearing gave the beholder to understand that they were persons of distinction. From the other chariot alighted, first a man of middle age, next a woman somewhat younger, then an aged man and woman, the latter alighting with great elasticity of step. The countenance of this lady gave evidence that it had once been the throne of rare beauty.

"Why looketh my brother so thoughtful and sad on this day of general rejoicing in Judah?" asked the aged lady, directing her address to one of those who had alighted from the first chariot.

"I am not sad, sister," replied the brother, "but am thoughtful. And what thinkest thou my mind dwelt upon?"

"Surely, I cannot tell. Some past scenes in Chaldea, peradventure."

"Nay, sister. But I was thinking that seventy and two years ago this very night, myself and my two brothers here, accompanied by our beloved Jeremiah, entered this house, and revealed the sad story of our captivity to our beloved Perreeza."

"Ah, dear Hananiah! and a dark night of sorrow that proved to your almost brokenhearted sister."

"But I trust that Jehovah hath overruled the whole in the end to the glory of his great name," said Mishael.

"Surely he hath!" quickly answered Mathias. "Forever blessed be the memory of that delightful night when these eyes, at the house of Barzello, rested on the bright charms of the 'Rose of Sharon.'"

"The rose no longer blooms, Mathias!" answered Perreeza. "It's hues are faded; and, under the pelting storms of life, its petals have well-nigh withered."

"The tint may fade, and the petals may wither, but sweeter than ever shall its fragrance continue to perfume the surrounding air," answered the husband, his face glowing with pure affection. "In that better country whither we are going, where flowers never fade, and where roses forever bloom, the 'Rose of Sharon' shall yet flourish in immortal beauty."

Mathias, Perreeza and the latter's three brothers had been made almoners of an immense bequest provided in Joram's will for advancing the interests of Judah. It was stipulated that the fund should not be employed until the expiration of seventy years of captivity. Joram believed, with Daniel and the other distinguished Israelites, that the captivity would come to an end in the specified seventy years. The treasure was hidden where none but the almoners and their natural heirs could disturb it.

It was Esrom's purpose, as a final atonement, to bequeath one-half of his vast fortune for the development of religious and educational institutions in Jerusalem and to aid the poorer class of Hebrews to acquire homes. The decision of Cyrus the king to assist in rebuilding the Temple at Jerusalem enabled Mathias and his associates to use the bequest in other channels. The fund at their disposal was large, and they were enabled to give a new impetus to the cause of education in Judah. Hundreds of the former captives were likewise assisted in the purchase of land and cattle. Much had been accomplished in the past year for the upbuilding of Jerusalem and the advancement of the race. It was natural, therefore, that, at the close of the ceremonies attending the laying of the foundation of the new temple, Esrom's friends should let their minds dwell on his generosity. Conversation turned to this theme as the family entered their home.

"It was a gracious and noble thing for Joram to do,"

exclaimed Hananiah.

"My uncle frequently told me," said Perreeza, "that it was his earnest desire to have his native city and his beloved land of Judah take a more advanced position in the affairs of the world. He believed that, with higher educational advantages, the Israelites would rapidly gain in statecraft. They are an industrious people, and many of them have shown such marked administrative ability as to convince observing men that the race will be potent in shaping the destiny of nations.

"Uncle Esrom became the wealthiest man in all Babylon because of his sagacity in barter and exchange. He was wise in regard to what the populace would buy most freely and where to obtain the merchandise to the best advantage."

"His discretion rather than his wealth gave him influence at the king's court," exclaimed Mishael. "Joram was a credit to his people, and methinks he was remarkable for his talent as a diplomat. He had great influence in foreign countries, and his knowledge gained abroad was of the highest importance to Nebuchadnezzar throughout his reign. Our uncle never forgot his native land, and constantly exerted a powerful influence in behalf of the people of Judah. That work was secret and mysterious, however. Frequently we heard of unexpected concessions and favors to our people from the king, and in time found out that they were due to Joram's promptings."

"My great hope at present is," returned Perreeza, "to be spared long enough to see substantial fruit spring from Uncle Esrom's bounty."

"I second that hope," said Hananiah. "I wish to see all the returned captives well provided for. The children of all these families must have doubled advantages as a measure of restitution. We can accomplish much with the immense sum at our disposal."

"We ought now, under such favorable circumstances," said Mishael, "to give Israel a new start in commerce and education. We have the benefit of Daniel's wisdom in this great undertaking; for, on several occasions before we left Babylon, he outlined plans by which Joram's wishes might be carried out in a practical manner. With the present government of Chaldea to protect our nation, the security of life and property is assured. We can push our projects as hard as we please, and feel confident that nothing but good is being accomplished."

The melodious voice of young Rebekah was now heard in another apartment, warbling one of her sweetest songs.

"Jehovah bless the child!" cried the grandmother. "How that voice of melody cheers my heart!"

"Mother!" quickly replied Monroah. "Permit me to call her into this apartment, where she may sing and play thy favorite 'song of Judah.'"

"Thou art ever kind to thy mother, dear Monroah; do as thou desirest."

Rebekah was called.

"Will my daughter sing and play for us her grandmother's favorite 'song of Judah'?"

"With pleasure, mother," cried Rebekah, as she quickly left the apartment.

In a moment she returned, bearing in her arms a stringed instrument with which the reader is somewhat familiar, and proceeded with the following appropriate song:

*"When we our weary limbs to rest*
*Sat down by proud Euphrates' stream,*
*We wept, with doleful thoughts oppressed,*
*And Zion was our mournful theme.*

*"Our harps, that when with joy we sung*
*Were wont their tuneful parts to bear,*
*With silent strings neglected hung*
*On willow trees that withered there.*

*"Oh, Salem! once our happy seat,*
*When I of thee forgetful prove,*
*Then let my trembling hand forget*
*These speaking strings with art to move!*

*"Again we hail the sacred hall,*
*That echoed to our youthful lays!*
*And Amonober's children all*
*Have reached their home to end their days.*

*"To thee, Almighty King of kings,*
*In new-made hymns my voice I'll raise,*
*And instruments of many strings*
*Shall help me to adore and praise.*

*"How sweet to die in Judah's dale,*
*And with the fathers calmly rest;*
*The thought of sleeping in yon vale,*

*How soothing to my throbbing breast!*

*"A few more days of grief and pain,*
*And then adieu to every gloom,*
*For soon we all shall meet again,*
*Beyond the portals of the tomb."*

The old harp of Judah has also returned from the captivity, and is once more safely lodged in its own native Jerusalem, whence Esrom bore it to the land of strangers a century before.

Time has left some impression on its aged frame, but its tones are sweeter than ever. In that family it is held as a priceless treasure; and its melody shall sweetly fall on ears yet unborn, when the hands that now so skillfully sweep its well-tuned strings shall be palsied, and the sweet voices that blend with its thrilling chords shall be silent in the grave.

# Choose from Thousands of 1stWorldLibrary Classics By

Adolphus WilliamWard
Aesop
Agatha Christie
Alexander Aaronsohn
Alexander Kielland
Alexandre Dumas
Alfred Gatty
Alfred Ollivant
Alice Duer Miller
Alice Turner Curtis
Alice Dunbar
Ambrose Bierce
Amelia E. Barr
Andrew Lang
Andrew McFarland Davis
Anna Sewell
Annie Besant
Annie Hamilton Donnell
Annie Payson Call
Anton Chekhov
Arnold Bennett
Arthur Conan Doyle
Arthur Ransome
Atticus
B. M. Bower
Basil King
Bayard Taylor
Ben Macomber
Booth Tarkington
Bram Stoker
C. Collodi
C. E. Orr
C. M. Ingleby
Carolyn Wells
Catherine Parr Traill
Charles A. Eastman
Charles Dickens
Charles Dudley Warner
Charles Farrar Browne
Charles Ives
Charles Kingsley
Charles Lathrop Pack
Charles Whibley
Charles Willing Beale
Charlotte M. Braeme
Charlotte M.Yonge
Clair W. Hayes
Clarence Day Jr.
Clarence E. Mulford

Clemence Housman
Confucius
Cornelis DeWitt Wilcox
Cyril Burleigh
D. H. Lawrence
Daniel Defoe
David Garnett
Don Carlos Janes
Donald Keyhole
Dorothy Kilner
Dougan Clark
E. Nesbit
E.P.Roe
E. Phillips Oppenheim
Edgar Allan Poe
Edgar Rice Burroughs
Edith Wharton
Edward J. O'Biren
John Cournos
Edwin L. Arnold
Eleanor Atkins
Elizabeth Cleghorn
Gaskell
Elizabeth Von Arnim
Ellem Key
Emily Dickinson
Erasmus W. Jones
Ernie Howard Pie
Ethel Turner
Ethel Watts Mumford
Eugenie Foa
Eugene Wood
Evelyn Everett-Green
Everard Cotes
F. J. Cross
Federick Austin Ogg
Ferdinand Ossendowski
Francis Bacon
Francis Darwin
Frances Hodgson Burnett
Frank Gee Patchin
Frank Harris
Frank Jewett Mather
Frank L. Packard
Frederick Trevor Hill
Frederick Winslow Taylor
Friedrich Kerst
Friedrich Nietzsche
Fyodor Dostoyevsky

Gabrielle E. Jackson
Garrett P. Serviss
Gaston Leroux
George Ade
Geroge Bernard Shaw
George Ebers
George Eliot
George MacDonald
George Orwell
George Tucker
George W. Cable
George Wharton James
Gertrude Atherton
Grace E. King
Grant Allen
Guillermo A. Sherwell
Gulielma Zollinger
Gustav Flaubert
H. A. Cody
H. B. Irving
H. G. Wells
H. H. Munro
H. Irving Hancock
H. Rider Haggard
H. W. C. Davis
Hamilton Wright Mabie
Hans Christian Andersen
Harold Avery
Harold McGrath
Harriet Beecher Stowe
Harry Houidini
Helent Hunt Jackson
Helen Nicolay
Hendy David Thoreau
Henrik Ibsen
Henry Adams
Henry Ford
Henry Frost
Henry James
Henry Jones Ford
Henry Seton Merriman
Henry Wadsworth
Longfellow
Henry W Longfellow
Herbert A. Giles
Herbert N. Casson
Herman Hesse
Homer
Honore De Balzac

Horace Walpole
Horatio Alger, Jr.
Howard Pyle
Howard R. Garis
Hugh Lofting
Hugh Walpole
Humphry Ward
Ian Maclaren
Israel Abrahams
J.G.Austin
J. Henri Fabre
J. M. Barrie
J. Macdonald Oxley
J. S. Knowles
J. Storer Clouston
Jack London
Jacob Abbott
James Allen
James Lane Allen
James Andrews
James Baldwin
James DeMille
James Joyce
James Oliver Curwood
James Oppenheim
James Otis
Jane Austen
Jens Peter Jacobsen
Jerome K. Jerome
John Burroughs
John F. Kennedy
John Gay
John Glasworthy
John Habberton
John Joy Bell
John Milton
John Philip Sousa
Jonathan Swift
Joseph Carey
Joseph Conrad
Joseph Jacobs
Julian Hawthrone
Julies Vernes
Justin Huntly McCarthy
Kakuzo Okakura
Kenneth Grahame
Kate Langley Bosher
L. A. Abbot
L. T. Meade
L. Frank Baum
Laura Lee Hope

Laurence Housman
Leo Tolstoy
Leonid Andreyev
Lewis Carroll
Lilian Bell
Lloyd Osbourne
Louis Tracy
Louisa May Alcott
Lucy Fitch Perkins
Lucy Maud Montgomery
Lydia Miller Middleton
Lyndon Orr
M. H. Adams
Margaret E. Sangster
Margaret Vandercook
Maria Edgeworth
Maria Thompson Daviess
Mariano Azuela
Marion Polk Angellotti
Mark Overton
Mark Twain
Mary Austin
Mary Cole
Mary Rowlandson
Mary Wollstonecraft
Shelley
Max Beerbohm
Myra Kelly
Nathaniel Hawthrone
O. F. Walton
Oscar Wilde
Owen Johnson
P.G.Wodehouse
Paul and Mable Thorn
Paul G. Tomlinson
Paul Severing
Peter B. Kyne
Plato
R. Derby Holmes
R. L. Stevenson
Rabindranath Tagore
Rahul Alvares
Ralph Waldo Emmerson
Rene Descartes
Rex E. Beach
Richard Harding Davis
Richard Jefferies
Robert Barr
Robert Frost
Robert Gordon Anderson
Robert L. Drake

Robert Lansing
Robert Michael Ballantyne
Robert W. Chambers
Rosa Nouchette Carey
Ross Kay
Rudyard Kipling
Samuel B. Allison
Samuel Hopkins Adams
Sarah Bernhardt
Selma Lagerlof
Sherwood Anderson
Sigmund Freud
Standish O'Grady
Stanley Weyman
Stella Benson
Stephen Crane
Stewart Edward White
Stijn Streuvels
Swami Abhedananda
Swami Parmananda
T. S. Ackland
The Princess Der Ling
Thomas A. Janvier
Thomas A Kempis
Thomas Anderton
Thomas Bailey Aldrich
Thomas Bulfinch
Thomas De Quincey
Thomas H. Huxley
Thomas Hardy
Thomas More
Thornton W. Burgess
U. S. Grant
Valentine Williams
Victor Appleton
Virginia Woolf
Walter Scott
Washington Irving
Wilbur Lawton
Wilkie Collins
Willa Cather
Willard F. Baker
William Makepeace
Thackeray
William W. Walter
Winston Churchill
Yei Theodora Ozaki
Young E. Allison
Zane Grey